One Hot
SCANDAL

Other Books by Anna Durand

One Hot
SCANDAL

Hot Brits, Book Seven

ANNA DURAND

JACOBSVILLE BOOKS JB MARIETTA, OHIO`

ONE HOT SCANDAL

ISBN: 978-1-934631-32-4 (paperback)
ISBN: 978-1-934631-11-9 (ebook)
ISBN: 978-1-934631-55-3 (audiobook)

Manufactured in the United States.

Jacobsville Books
www.JacobsvilleBooks.com

Publisher's Cataloging-in-Publication Data
provided by Five Rainbows Cataloging Services

Names: Durand, Anna.
Title: One hot scandal / Anna Durand.
Description: Marietta, OH : Jacobsville Books, 2022. | Series: Hot Brits, bk. 7.
Identifiers: ISBN 978-1-934631-32-4 (paperback) | ISBN 978-1-934631-11-9 (ebook) | ISBN 978-1-934631-55-3 (audiobook)
Subjects: LCSH: Man-woman relationships--Fiction. | Aristocracy (Social class)--Fiction. | Scandals--Fiction. | British--Fiction. | Americans--Fiction. | Romance fiction. | BISAC: FICTION / Romance / Contemporary. | FICTION / Romance / Romantic Comedy. | GSAFD: Love stories.
Classification: LCC PS3604.U724 O545 2022 (print) | LCC PS3604.U724 (ebook) | DDC 813/.6--dc23.

Chapter One

Hugh

I tilt my chair back and stare up at the tiles on the ceiling of my office, wondering how I managed to cock my life up so thoroughly. I used to love my life, but now I need to hide in my office to avoid causing any further damage—not just to me, but to my family. It all started when I flew to Scotland to help my best mate, Callum MacTaggart, get through a rough patch. Then I met the woman of my dreams and promptly lost her—to my best friend. Ever since, I've been a bit…off my game.

My desk phone rings.

I snatch it up. "Yes, Trudy?"

"Your mother is on line one," my executive assistant says. "Lady Sommerleigh is quite insistent. Should I tell her you're indisposed again?"

"No. Put her through."

After a pause, I hear my mother's voice. "Hugh, how are you this morning?"

"Fine, Mum. Did you ring me to ask what I ate for breakfast?"

"No, dear."

She sighs with the sort of motherly exasperation that means she's about to order me to get my chin up and act like a viscount. However we viscounts are meant to behave. But she doesn't chastise me. Yet.

"Listen to me, Hugh. What I'm about to say are the most important words I have ever spoken to you." She pauses, and just when I think we've gotten disconnected, she speaks again. "You have made a bloody mess of your life. It's time to get your chin up, stiffen your upper lip, and stop behaving like a chancer."

I glance around the office, looking for a hidden camera. She must be pulling a prank on me. The Viscountess Sommerleigh never speaks to anyone the way she just spoke to me. But of course, there are no cameras. She is not joking. "Mum, what are you on about?"

"You haven't been yourself lately. I don't approve of your behavior, but you are a grown man who can make his own decisions about his life."

"Thank you. Are we done now?"

"No." She speaks the word so sharply that I instinctively snap up straight in my chair. "Ruining your own life is bad enough. But you have brought shame to the Sommerleigh title and to your family. That I cannot stand for."

Now I'm squirming in my chair. Though I wish I could deny what she just said, I can't. It's all true. She had told me the same thing on more than one occasion recently, in person, but I don't enjoy hearing it again. "I'm sorry, Mum. I never meant for any of that to happen, but there are circumstances—"

"Shut up, Hugh. I am not finished."

I freeze. Pretty sure my jaw drops. I sit here like a statue while I wait for my mother to share the rest. Considering how she's scolded me so far, I'm fairly certain I don't want to hear more. But I deserve whatever she's about to tell me.

"You need help," Mum says. "I'm doing this for your own good. Please remember that, and remember who you are—the Viscount Sommerleigh, successor to a title that was once revered."

"I know. I'm sorry for embarrassing you, honestly. I won't do it again."

"Oh, Hugh, it's too late for apologies to matter."

What can I say to that? Nothing. My father had been a true aristocrat, a gentleman of the first order, the sort who never said the wrong thing or did the wrong thing. I have dishonored his memory, but not on purpose.

"I'm sending you a gift," Mum says. "Obedience is required."

Obedience? To a gift? My behavior must have driven my mother insane because she seems to be spouting nonsense—or as the Scots would say, her bum's oot the windae. "I don't understand. What sort of gift is it?"

"You'll see. Goodbye, dear."

My mother hangs up on me.

I slump in my chair. What just happened? I'm receiving a gift. Can't imagine why Mum would reward me for shaming the family and the Sommerleigh title.

My desk phone rings again. "What now, Trudy?"

She clears her throat. "Well, um, there's a woman here to see you. She says your mother sent her."

"What does she want?" I'm in no mood to talk to anyone. Maybe I should go home and sleep for a century or so, until everyone has forgotten what an arse I am.

"I'm not sure," Trudy says. "But she insists on seeing you immediately."

"Fine. Send her in." I sit up straighter and take a deep breath, steeling myself against whatever might come next.

The door opens, and a beautiful brunette walks into my office. Her hips sway slightly, and the modest heels she wears show off her slender ankles. As she approaches the chair in front of my desk, I can't stop myself from admiring the swell of her hips and the mounds of her breasts, though her businesswoman outfit doesn't let me see much of those mounds. Her cleavage teases me with only a glimpse of their slopes.

She leans over my desk just enough to offer me her hand to shake. "Good morning, Lord Sommerleigh. I'm Avery Hahn."

The sexy woman is American.

I rise from my chair and shake her hand. "Good morning, Miss Hahn."

"Ms. Hahn, not Miss." She settles her shapely arse onto the chair. Only now do I realize she holds two objects in her left hand—a small brown purse and a matching leather portfolio. "Please take a seat, Lord Sommerleigh. We have a great deal to discuss."

"Have we?" I sit down. "What can I do for you?"

It's more a question of what I can do *to* her, but I shouldn't be thinking about sex. Mum was right. I need to change my behavior.

Avery Hahn sets her purse on the floor and lays the leather port-folio on her thigh. Then she flips the posh folder open, plucking a ballpoint pen out of it. She taps the tip of that pen on the pad of paper inside her portfolio. "Your mother hired me to fix you."

"Fix me? I don't understand."

"You have made a fool of yourself and become a laughingstock. Is that how you want the world to see the Viscount Sommerleigh?"

"No, of course not. But I can manage my life on my own. Don't need your help. No offense."

"You can't offend me. I've heard everything in my line of work." She tips her head to the side and seems to be studying me. "Why do you call yourself Lord Steamy?"

"I didn't invent the nickname. Some silly bird coined it."

"But you do use the name when you're flirting with women. Correct?"

How does she know that? Well, Mum sent her, so… *Bloody hell*. Did someone tell my mother about that?

"I'll take your silence as a yes."

While she goes on staring at me, I notice the color of her eyes. They're so blue they seem almost purple. I've never seen eyes that shade be-fore. It's stunning. *She* is stunning, from her fingernails that are painted a pale shade of pink to her hip-hugging skirt and those perfect lips. She painted them a deep burgundy, which makes me want to kiss her for some reason. I want to kiss every beautiful woman I meet, so I suppose it's no mystery why I feel that way now.

But that impulse might be part of my problem.

Avery jots something down on her notepad.

"What are you writing there?" I ask.

"Notes about you, of course." She crosses her legs, which makes her skirt ride up a sliver, showing off more of her creamy skin. "What did Lady Sommerleigh tell you?"

"That she was sending me a gift." I can't help eying her with a touch of suspicion. "What exactly did Mum tell you to do with me?"

"Your reputation is in tatters. I'm here to save it."

I notice she didn't say she means to save *me*. She plans on saving "it," as in the reputation of the sodding Viscount Sommerleigh. "Since I never had a reputation to start with, you are wasting your time."

"Oh, no, you can't chase me away. Your mother insisted I need to stick to you like glue until you can show your face in public again without embarrassing yourself, your family, or the Sommerleigh name." She pulls a folded sheet of paper out of a pocket in her portfolio. "You can't escape your mistakes, Lord Sommerleigh."

"Please stop calling me that. I'm just Hugh."

"Afraid I can't use your first name. Lady Sommerleigh was explicit in her instructions to me. I will refer to you only as Lord Sommerleigh."

"I have no say about what you call me? That's rubbish."

She unfolds that bloody sheet of paper, smooths it out on her lap, then holds it up for me to see.

Oh, bollocks. It's a photocopy of a tabloid headline and the article beneath it—"Lord Steamy Cuckolds the Duke of Wackenbourne." Perhaps I did do that, but I don't like seeing the headline again. Why should anyone give a toss about a measly viscount accidentally sleeping with a duke's wife? Benedict Pemberton-Rice has shagged his way through most of the bedrooms in London, sleeping with the wives of far more important men than the Duke of Wackenbourne himself.

"Why did you seduce the Duke's wife?" Avery asks. "I've been led to believe you're a smart man, but you did something very, very stupid."

"Yes, I know. But I had no idea who she was." I wince because I suddenly feel as if someone has put nettles in my chair. "I met Annabelle at a pub in the middle of bloody nowhere, and she never told me her last name or that she was married. I do not seduce other men's wives."

"But you have one-nighters with strange women and don't bother to ask their full names."

"No, that's not—Honestly, this is none of your concern." I rise and point toward the door. "Thank you for coming, Ms. Hahn, but it's time you left. I do not need your help."

Still not sure what exactly Mum hired her to do, but I absolutely do not need whatever it is.

Avery wags a finger at me. "Now, now, Lord Sommerleigh. That's no way for a peer to behave."

"Are you a psychotherapist?"

"No."

"You must be a lawyer, then."

"No." She stands up and approaches my desk, then balances her lovely arse on its edge. "I'm an image consultant."

"A what? I've never heard of that." I gesture at my clothing. "And I don't need help with dressing myself."

She leans over the desk, planting one hand on the surface right over my calendar. "I'm here to repair your public image and make you respectable again."

"I'm fine the way I am."

"Maybe you don't give a damn about what people think of you, but your behavior has harmed more than your reputation. You are the CEO of Sommerleigh Sweets, an international candy manufacturer. How do you think your dispute with the Duke of Wackenbourne has affected your company? Not in a good way, that's how."

I bar my arms over my chest. "Why don't you type up a list of things you want me to do and say, and I will follow your instructions to the letter."

"Uh-uh. That won't do." She slides off my desk. "I'm under strict orders to stick to you like glue, remember? You can't scare me away. I've dealt with every kind of jackass in my profession, and you are nothing compared to the rest of them. Might as well give up and let me do my job. You don't want to disappoint your mother, do you?"

Oh, that's a dirty trick. But she's right about my image being somewhat tarnished these days. I slump down onto my chair and resign myself to the inevitable. "All right. Tell me how this is meant to work."

"You follow my orders. That's how it works."

I might like to hear a woman say that in bed, but I don't feel excited by the prospect of letting a stranger order me around while repairing my image. I blow out a sigh. "How do we start?"

"You are going to tell me everything about yourself." Avery smirks. "And I mean absolutely everything, including all your dirty little secrets."

I rest an elbow on my chair's arm, drop my face into my raised hand, and groan.

Chapter Two

Avery

Hugh Parrish is nothing like what I expected. Most of my clients are either angry or ashamed, and they always fight the process from beginning to end. Hugh is both angry and ashamed, yet he still agreed to cooperate. I also expected a viscount to be dressed just so, but his tie is slightly askew, his dark hair seems like he forgot to comb it this morning, and his eyes are faintly red. I doubt he realizes he looks that way. The man seems frazzled.

Lord Sommerleigh has several factors going for him when it comes to polishing up his image. He's attractive and sexy, but also smart and accomplished. The man runs an international corporation. By all accounts, he does an excellent job. Though I haven't experienced his infamous charisma yet, Lady Sommerleigh had informed me that her son does have a charming side. She also warned me that Hugh hasn't quite been himself lately. She couldn't explain why.

Now I need to find out the answer. Lady Sommerleigh did give me clues, though I doubt she realized that.

"How do we start?" he asks with all the enthusiasm of a man-whore about to be condemned to a life sentence in a monastery.

"You tell me every last thing I want to know." I glance around the big office, with its floor-to-ceiling windows and designer furniture. "Would you be more comfortable doing this in a relaxed setting, away from work?"

"Not sure it matters where we do this." He lowers his hand, leaning his head back against his chair. "Just get on with it."

"When did you last have sex?"

"How is that any of your business?"

"Told you. I need to know everything."

The Viscount Sommerleigh scowls at me. "My sex life is out of bounds."

"Afraid not. You gave up your right to privacy on the night you seduced a duke's wife." I settle onto the chair I'd been sitting in a moment ago and grab my portfolio, pen poised above the paper. "Why were you hanging around in a backwater pub in the middle of the northern English countryside? It's nowhere near Sommerleigh."

He puckers his lips and narrows his gaze.

Does he honestly think I've never seen the Stubborn Jackass look before? I could write a book on the subject. Instead of giving him what he wants—to annoy me, or at least to provoke me into asking more questions that will annoy him—I relax in my chair and gaze at him with a neutral expression.

When I cross my legs casually, his attention flicks down to my knees. He slides his tongue over his lips. The man is attracted to me. But that won't help him wriggle out of answering my questions.

"You're right," he says, his voice deeper and huskier. "We should go somewhere else to do this."

The man-whore wants to screw me. Like I've never experienced that phenomenon before. Male clients can't help it. Their libidos always get the better of them, and they wind up hitting on me. A few women have tried the same thing. But I don't sleep with any of my clients.

Still, when Hugh spoke in that husky tone, I felt a delicious little flutter in my tummy. Yes, I've experienced that phenomenon too. I'm only human, so of course I've suffered the odd twinge of attraction. Sexy, powerful men turn me on. Hugh doesn't seem to realize that he is powerful, in terms of his position in society and as the Viscount Sommerleigh, not to mention the fact he runs a corporation. Maybe his lack of self-awareness is part of his problem.

"Here is just fine," I tell him. "Answer my question. Why were you in a backwater pub—"

"Because I was thirsty. Have you asked Annabelle Pemberton-Rice why she was there?"

"No, and I don't plan to speak to her or the Duke. They are irrelevant to my job." Since he's clearly attracted to me, I decide to leverage that for my purposes. I uncross my legs, then cross them again, drawing his attention back to my body. "I need the truth, Lord Sommerleigh. Can't help you unless I know everything."

He taps a finger on his lips as he continues to admire my legs. "I was driving home from a trip to Scotland. The Highlands. A little village called Loch Fairbairn, to be precise."

"Why were you in Scotland? Was it a vacation?"

"Didn't Mum tell you?"

"She said you went to visit your best friend, who is Scottish. But she didn't know anything else, except that you seemed different when you came home."

"I am different." His gaze lowers as if he's staring at the floor. For a moment, he just sits there with a strangely melancholy expression. Then he straightens and aims his pale-blue eyes directly at me. "But none of that is your concern. I will not discuss my time in Scotland. Understand? It's off limits."

Okay, I've pushed him as far as I can for today. Time to move on to another subject. "Tell me about your job."

"What has that got to do with anything?"

I shrug. "Won't know until you tell me."

Hugh picks up his desk phone and punches buttons on it. "Trudy, would you please give Ms. Hahn our standard informational packet? Thank you." As he hangs up the phone, he smirks. "Soon you will know everything you never wanted to know about Sommerleigh Sweets."

"That's not what I meant, and you know it. A brochure—"

"Is all you'll get from me today." He rises, tugs his jacket down, and offers me his hand. "Good day, Ms. Hahn."

Jeez, his mood changed in an instant. Whatever happened in Scotland is clearly the source of his problems. But since he won't talk about it yet, I opt for a strategic and temporary withdrawal. This is war, and I'll need to fight many battles to get the job done.

So I get up and shake his hand. "We'll be seeing each other again very soon, Lord Sommerleigh."

He lays a hand over his heart and adopts a look of sarcastic desire. "Oh, I can't wait for that. You have stolen my heart, Ms. Hahn. Don't leave me for too long."

Though I try not to, I can't help smiling just a little. He is likable. And sexy. And smart. I've always been a sucker for men like that. But I never get involved with a client.

I walk out of Hugh's office.

Then I go back to the huge hotel suite Lady Sommerleigh had arranged for me. It's the biggest suite in the fanciest hotel in London, which means it's much too big for one person. But I can't complain. I have a jacuzzi in the bathroom and a bed so soft I could practically have an orgasm just from lying on it.

Lady Sommerleigh had been explicit in her instructions to me—fix Hugh at any cost. I will succeed, despite his behavior today.

I change out of my work clothes and into my favorite satin pajamas. They're sky blue with puffy white clouds on them. Yes, I enjoy wearing silly PJs, though nobody else knows about that since I live alone. I might be a hard-ass at work, but I like to feel girlie in my off hours. I also like to indulge in the occasional junk meal, which is my term for anything I eat that doesn't involve vegetables or have a high fiber count. Though it's only mid-afternoon, I order room service and request a sirloin steak, a baked potato with all the trimmings, and an extra-large slice of coconut cream pie.

Just as I'm shoving the first forkful of pie into my mouth, my cell phone rings. I check the caller ID, then answer with my mouth full. "Hello, Derek."

"I think you said hello, but I can't be sure. Sounds like you just got home from the dentist. Did one of your clients deck you and crack your teeth?"

"Ha-ha." I wipe my mouth and set my plate of pie on the end table. "Why are you up so early? It's not even noon yet in your neck of the woods."

"Just wanted to check in on my baby sister. Don't get to see you much anymore, what with all your traveling." He sighs. "I wouldn't mind if you were off having fun on a tropical beach."

"No time for that. My services are in high demand."

"Yeah, I know, and I'm proud of your success. But I miss you. With Mom and Dad gone, all we've got is each other."

"I miss you too. Promise I'll be home for Thanksgiving this year."

Maybe I have missed every major holiday for the past two years, but I can't help that my job often requires me to take off at a moment's notice. My clients need help urgently. My brother has never understood that. When scandal strikes, the rich and powerful need someone like me.

But Hugh Parrish doesn't seem like the rich-and-powerful type. He's more middle-of-the-road wealthy. I know that because Lady Sommerleigh told me. She wanted me to have all the boring details about her son before I took on the task of crawling under his skin to root out the cause of his current problem—aka, the Duke of Wackenbourne scandal.

"Which asshat who has more money than God are you helping this time?" Derek asks.

"God doesn't have money. He has no need for it."

"Don't get snarky with me. I'm seriously worried about my sister."

"Sure you are." I tuck my feet under me cross-legged and sneak another bite of pie before I speak again. "Do you think I can't handle myself?"

"No, of course you can. That's not the point."

I devour a huge mouthful of pie, getting whipped cream all over my chin. "Tell me what you've been up to since I left for London."

"You just left yesterday. I ate, slept, showered, and ate again. Are you going to tell me about your client?"

"You know I can't do that. Client information is confidential."

"Okay. I'll get online and look up London tabloids. That oughta give me a clue."

I laugh. "Do you have any idea how many scandals there are in this city? In this country? Rich Brits have a way of getting tangled up in sticky situations and becoming the objects of gossip."

"Well, at least tell me if your client is a man or a woman."

"No way. You will not use my job as a makeshift matchmaking enterprise."

Derek laughs so loudly I swear I can hear the spittle flying from his lips. "I don't need any help getting dates. It's you I worry about. When was the last time you got laid, Avery?"

"We don't talk about sex, remember? It's too weird."

"Not asking for a play-by-play. Just wondering if you're so obsessed with work that you forget to make time for the good things in life. Everybody needs to cut loose now and then." His voice drops to a sarcastic whisper. "I won't tell anybody you eat with your mouth full. What kind of pie is it, anyway?"

I stare at my loaded fork. "How did you know…"

"Because I'm your brother. I know how much you love to stuff your face, and you answered the phone with your mouth full. Only pie ever inspires you to pig out." He clears his throat and speaks in an imperious voice. "I grant you my permission to put your head in the pie trough and vacuum up all the coconut cream."

"You're mixing metaphors. And what makes you think it's coconut cream?"

He chuckles. "Known you all your life, Avery. Coconut cream is your favorite pie."

"I need to get back to work."

"Of course you do."

Why do I feel guilty about working hard? Only my brother every makes me feel that way. "I'll talk to you later. Goodbye, Derek."

I hang up on him. He doesn't mind when I do that. I did say goodbye, after all.

Now that I've fed my cravings, I need to devise a plan. Somehow, some way, I will get under Hugh Parrish's skin and convince him to share his secrets with me. It's my job, and I have never given up on a client. Lady Sommerleigh gave me Hugh's address here in London, so maybe I should go over there and try talking to him in a more relaxed setting.

Yes, that sounds like a reasonable plan.

I call Hugh's office, but only because I know his executive assistant will answer. "Trudy, hi, it's Avery Hahn."

"What can I do for you, Ms. Hahn?"

"Is Lord Sommerleigh still there?"

"No, he left early today, which isn't like him at all. I do worry about him lately."

"Relax, I'll take care of Lord Sommerleigh. Got any idea where he went?"

"Home, he said. 'Home as in my flat, not Sommerleigh.' Those were his exact words."

"Okay. Thank you, Trudy. You're a gem."

I hang up, then hurry into the bedroom to change clothes. No, I won't wear a business suit this time. I want Hugh to feel relaxed, so he'll be more open to talking, and that means I need to dress appropriately.

The Viscount Sommerleigh won't know what hit him.

Chapter Three

Hugh

I left work early, in the middle of the afternoon. Hugh Parrish, the Viscount Sommerleigh, does not do that. Blood hell, now I'm referring to myself by my title in my own head. Yes, I definitely have problems to work out, but Mum should not have hired an image consultant without, ah, consulting me.

What a whingeing arse I've become.

At least I won't see Avery Hahn again today. I need to stay celibate until the Wackenbourne scandal fades away, but Avery is the sexiest woman I've ever seen, even sexier than Kate Wagner. Kate didn't want me, but Avery does. If I have to spend every day with my image consultant, I will break my celibacy vow. It doesn't help that she likes to issue commands because a bossy woman has always been my sexual Achilles' heel. I have a lot of Achilles' heels when it comes to the ladies.

Yes, I love women. What's wrong with that?

Shagging a duke's wife, that's what, you bloody stupid arse.

I've just stepped out of the shower in my flat when the doorbell rings. *Oh, bollocks.* I wanted time alone, but instead, some wanker has decided to harass me at home. It's probably another tabloid reporter looking for an exclusive, which means a picture of Lord Steamy shagging someone else's wife.

The impatient visitor rings the doorbell again.

Slinging a towel around my hips, I jog out to the front door and check the little screen that displays the security camera feed. Yes, I've learned my lesson about answering the door without checking who's out there first.

It's Avery Hahn.

Perfect. A beautiful, sexy woman wants to see me while I'm half-naked and haven't had sex in far too long. Maybe if I don't answer, she'll think I've gone somewhere else.

"Come on, Lord Sommerleigh," she says. "The doorman told me you're home. No point in pretending you aren't."

Will she ever stop calling me by my title?

Since I have no choice, I pull the door open partway. "What do you want? I'm not at the office, which means you have no right to harass me."

"I work twenty-four seven for my clients." Avery skims her gaze over me from head to toe, starting with my chest. She licks her lips, then clears her throat and looks me in the eye. "We need to talk. I can wait in the living room while you get dressed."

"Bugger off."

"No, Lord Sommerleigh, I won't go away." She folds her arms over her chest, which lifts her tits. "Might as well surrender. You can't out-stubborn me. Won't your mother be disappointed if you refuse to cooperate?"

Oh, now that is a low blow. Avery Hahn has no shame, does she?

I swing the door open and throw one arm wide. "Come in, mi-lady. Shall I roll out a velvet carpet for you to walk upon?"

"That won't be necessary."

She ambles into the flat, heading for the sofa in the living room.

And I finally notice what she's wearing—jeans, a casual white blouse, and canvas shoes with no socks. The security camera only showed me black and white. Her hair, which had been tied back in a crisp bun earlier, now flows over her shoulders in luscious waves. Her deep blue eyes seem to sparkle in the sunlight beaming through the picture windows.

Avery stops near the sofa, her lips curling into a slight smile as she takes in her surroundings. "You have a nice place, but I assumed it would be..."

"Filled with erotic art and statues of fertility gods? Afraid I left my pornographic video collection back at Sommerleigh."

"Stop assuming you know what I assume."

"That sounds like some sort of grammatical feedback loop." I shut the door but don't move, and I try like hell not to look at her body. Getting an erection in front of the woman who wants to repair my public image seems like a ruddy awful idea. "What are you trying to say, darling? I can't read minds."

And I hope she can't either. Otherwise, I'm completely buggered.

"I said you shouldn't assume you know what I assume."

"What does that mean?" I throw my hands up. "Can we not play these word games? I've had enough of that rubbish."

Avery stops blinking, her eyes wider now. Her lips fall open, and her gaze darts down to my hips. Then she veers her gaze to my face, only to glance down at my hips again.

I glance down there too. "Oh, bollocks!"

Yes, I dropped the towel. I'm giving Avery Hahn the full monty.

"Sorry," I say, rushing to snatch up the towel. But I can't quite get hold of it and wind up whipping it about like a lunatic. "Sorry. I'll, ah—Never mind."

I race for the bedroom with the towel flapping behind me like a flag.

When I return a moment later, dressed in khaki trousers and a light-blue polo shirt, Avery is sitting on the sofa with her hands clasped on her lap. She sits upright, her spine straight.

"That was an unfortunate accident," I tell her as I drop onto an armchair. "Honestly, I wasn't trying to seduce you."

She eyes me sideways. "I should hope not. If that's the best Lord Steamy can do, I'll be severely disappointed. I mean, with all the hype about you, I expected better than streaking in your own apartment."

I raise one hand, palm out. "On my father's grave, I swear it was an accident."

"A formal vow is unnecessary."

Can't resist leaning forward, giving her my patented sensual smile while I lower my voice to a deeper tone. "For the record, darling, I can do much better than streaking. Would you like a demonstration?"

"No thank you." Though she spoke in a curt tone, her lips have curled up slightly. "But I'm glad that's not the best you've got."

"I'll give you that demonstration anytime you like, love."

What the bloody hell am I doing? Seducing the wrong woman is what got me into trouble, so I will not try it on with Avery. Well, never again since I already did that—accidentally. Flirtation is a reflex.

"I'd rather talk about your image," Avery says. "That's why your mother hired me, after all."

"Do you live in the UK? You're obviously American, so I wondered."

"Maybe I'm Canadian. Ever think of that?"

"Well, ah…" No, I hadn't thought of that. My mate Logan MacTaggart can tell the difference between an American and a Canadian after hearing the person speak five syllables, but he used to be a spy. I'm just an average bloke.

Avery laughs, the sound light and gentle, almost teasing. "Relax, I was just giving you a hard time. I'm American. But no, I don't live in the UK. I go wherever my services are needed, which in this case means London. That's where my new client lives."

"Are you talking about me? I assume you have other clients here in the UK."

"Right now, you are my sole client. Lady Sommerleigh insisted that I manage your problem exclusively until it's settled."

Blimey. Mum is paying a beautiful woman to care for my needs and no one else's. I must be worse off than I realized. "How do you mean to settle my problem?"

"It's all about image. When I'm done, everyone will think you're squeaky clean and the perfect viscount."

"Perfect? Let's not overshoot the mark, darling. I'd settle for 'not a sodding arsehole.' "

"You aren't an asshole."

She tips her head side to side, squinting as if she's studying me with more intensity this time. Her attention makes me feel itchy, and I struggle to resist the urge to scratch my arms. Since she insists on scrutinizing me, I give in to the impulse to admire her body. Christ, I'd love to shag her. *Don't even think about it, you bloody moron.*

I can't control my thoughts, but I can shift my gaze away from her. Doing that takes a dismaying amount of self-control.

Avery glances at my feet. "You're not wearing shoes."

"No. Is that a problem? Should I wear shoes when I'm inside my own home as part of my image rehabilitation program?"

"I wasn't criticizing you. I'm surprised, that's all. Most of the aristocrats I've met would be horrified if anyone saw them without a tie on, much less no shoes."

"Yes, all peers share the same likes and dislikes. We're identical in every way. Might as well replace me with a robot replica."

She puckers her lips, but I think she's trying not to smile rather than preparing to chastise me.

I wave toward her feet. "Feel free to kick your shoes off. I won't tell anyone you did it."

Avery isn't wearing socks, which suggests she isn't as rigid as she seemed in my office earlier. Her entire demeanor has changed since the moment she walked into my flat. I liked her schoolmarm attitude, but this version of her makes me dangerously randy.

She kicks her shoes off and wriggles her toes. The nails are painted pink, naturally.

If I'd been dangerously randy a few seconds ago, now I'm about to get an erection. Her adorable little toes turn me on more than I would have expected. I'd love to suck on those digits—while we're naked. I don't have a general foot fetish, but some women love a good toe-sucking.

"That does feel better," she says with a smile as adorably sweet as her pink toenails. "Thank you, Lord Sommerleigh."

"For what?"

"Inviting me to take my shoes off."

"You're welcome to do that anytime in my presence."

Her brows lift as if she's waiting for me to say or do something. "Aren't you going to suggest I can take off other things in your presence too? You've been flirting with me, after all."

"Sorry. It's a reflex."

Avery rests her feet on the coffee table. "Are you ready to tell me everything about yourself? Can't help until you do."

"Why don't we have tea first? With biscuits, of course. That means cookies."

"I know. I might be American, but I'm not ignorant of everything British."

"Sorry. I didn't mean to insult you." I squirm in my chair, which is a ridiculous thing for a grown man to do. Avery makes me uncomfortable. "I assume that's a no to tea and biscuits."

"Actually, I'd love that. But we can talk about you while we wait for the tea."

"But I need to go into the kitchen to make it."

She hooks a thumb over her shoulder. "The kitchen is right there. I can sit at the bar while you make tea."

"I prefer to do that alone."

Avery hops to her feet and grabs my hand, tugging as if she wants me to get up. "Come on. It's more fun to do things like this with company."

This woman is relentless. Suddenly, I wish I'd chosen a flat with a separate kitchen rather than an open design. But I give in and push myself up and out of the chair. Avery sashays to the bar and rests her sexy arse on a stool while I walk around the other side to the kitchen counter. My nanny watches while I bring a teapot out of the cabinet.

"Why don't you heat the water in the microwave?" she asks. "It's faster."

"Microwave? Good lord, no. Mum must not have made tea for you when she was explaining what a disaster I am." I fill the teapot with water while I inform Avery, "Lady Sommerleigh would never have hired you if she knew what an American heathen you are."

She raises her hands. "Okay, I surrender. Do it the hard way. Tastes the same no matter how you heat up the water."

"It tastes the same?" I cluck my tongue, shaking my head at her. "You won't say that once you've had *my* tea."

"Uh-huh. I'm sure it'll rock my world."

Avery watches me for a bit longer while I wait for the water to boil, but she rests her elbow on the bar and cradles her chin in her upraised hand. Then she begins to drum her fingers on her cheek. After a few minutes of that, she excuses herself to "use the little girl's room." When I tell her the bathroom is inside the bedroom, she smirks. Should I worry about what that expression means?

By the time she returns, the tea has finished steeping.

"You were in the loo for a bloody long time," I say as I set two cups on the bar. "Having a problem, love?"

"No, I'm fine. But I took the opportunity to snoop in your bathroom."

"Is spying a standard part of your image repair arsenal?"

"Yes, but only when stubborn men refuse to talk to me."

"Hmm, I think I should be offended or perhaps enraged by that statement." I set the teapot on the bar. "Would you care for milk or sugar?"

"Both, please."

I pour a bit of milk into each cup, then add the tea. Avery doesn't complain about that. When I set a bowl of sugar on the bar, she snatches up the spoon I'd given her and proceeds to dump heaping spoonfuls of sugar into her cup. One. Two. Three. Four.

"That's enough," I say as I slap my palm over her cup to stop her from dumping any more sugar in there. "You'll never taste the tea if you keep doing that."

"Sugar is my weakness. And I haven't complained about the way you put milk in my cup first."

I lean across the bar and clasp her hands. "You are a heathen for sure, darling. But I love that about you."

"Wait until you see how I drink tea." She glances around the kitchen. "Got any straws?"

I cover my face with my hands and groan.

Chapter Four

Avery

Hugh is adorable when he's shocked. I don't really drink tea through a straw, but I do enjoy teasing him—more than I should. Though I never flirt with clients, I think I might've done that a moment ago, accidentally. He's much more relaxed at home, which will help me get through to him, but it also makes him far more appealing. I can understand why women love Hugh. He has an easy charm that seems completely natural, like it's embedded in his DNA.

Hugh finally lifts his gaze to mine. He gives me a wry smile, shaking his head, then turns toward the cabinets above the counter. Bringing out a box of biscuits, he carefully arranges several of them on a small plate.

While he's doing that, I survey his flat from the comfort of my stool. This is a luxury apartment, for sure, but that's no surprise. The kitchen features a marble bar that also serves as an island, plus a matching marble countertop. The whole place has a modern cream-colored palette, though the lower cabinets are a pale gray. The living room features built-in dark-wood shelving along one wall, but the rest of it sticks to the off-white theme, including the sofa.

But the bathroom... Whoa, mama, I could live in there.

I'd gone through the bedroom to reach the bathroom, so I got a good look at the huge bed Hugh sleeps in as well as the floor-to-ceiling windows with gauzy drapes. But the bathroom itself was what blew me away. Two marble sinks. A toilet encased in marble. Huge storage cabinets made of a pale wood. The towels hanging on the matching wood racks felt as soft as silk. The most stunning feature is the shower, which has no doors. The marble stall stands completely open while five showerheads occupy various spots on the three walls. Natural light pours through an adjacent window, muted slightly by tree branches outside.

Holy cow. I might sleep with Hugh just so I can use his shower.

No, I won't have sex with him. That was a casual thought, not an ardent desire.

Lord Sommerleigh places the plate of biscuits on the bar between our cups of tea. Then he saunters around to this side of the island and sits on the stool beside mine. "Now remember, darling. Dunk the biscuits. Don't drown them."

"What if I want to eat them dry?"

"That's not the proper British way." He daintily dunks a biscuit into his tea and bites off a small chunk. After chewing that, he takes a sip and repeats the process. "That's how it's done."

"No sugar?"

"I prefer my tea with milk only." He smirks at me. "But I have never seen anyone drown Earl Grey in sugar the way you do. Still want that straw?"

"No, I was kidding about that. But I honestly do love loads of sugar." I dive a biscuit into my tea and dunk it vigorously several times before I stuff the whole thing in my mouth. While still chewing, I say, "Have I shocked you again?"

"Revulsion would be a more appropriate word for it."

Now that I have him relaxed, it's time to start the inquisition. "So, tell me about the Duke of Wackenbourne."

"What about him? We're not mates. I met the man once."

"Yes, I know all about that. He crashed a garden party at Sommerleigh and slugged you in the gut, then punched you in the jaw. Your mother showed me a photo of your bruised face."

"It wasn't as bad as it looked. Wackenbourne shouted obscenities at me after that, and fortunately, he left without assaulting me any further."

"The Duke is in the House of Lords, right? In Parliament?"

"Yes."

"That means he has connections and power."

Hugh gives me an annoyed look. "There are over seven hundred members of the House of Lords. He's just another wanker with a seat in Parliament. No more or less powerful than most of the other members."

"Sure, but he hates you. The Duke has used his influence to try to ruin you."

"Ruin me?" Hugh chuckles, but it's a bitter sound. "I've done that smashingly on my own. What he's done is merely the icing on the cake."

"Are you ready to tell me about Scotland?"

He snaps a biscuit in half and tosses the pieces into his tea where they float on the surface. "Scotland is a region to the north of England and is part of the United Kingdom. People there love plaid and often wear kilts. They also enjoy haggis and bagpipe music."

"That's not what I meant, and you know it. Please tell me what happened the last time you visited Scotland."

"Bugger off, would you?"

He leaps off his stool and stalks over to the windows to glare out at the trees, shoving his hands into his pants pockets.

I pad over there too and stand beside him. "I know telling me to 'bugger off' is a rude thing to say. Don't insult me. I'm here to help you, but I can't do that if you refuse to cooperate."

"Are you my image consultant or my therapist?"

"Whatever you need me to be. Just don't get nasty again. Got it?"

"Sorry. I know I've been an arse." He rubs his eyes and sighs. "Scotland is...something I'm not ready to talk about yet."

"Fair enough." I lay a hand on his arm, feeling the firmness of his biceps. Wow, he's got nice muscles under that fancy polo shirt. "Maybe you can tell me about the Duke's wife instead."

"What about her? She's a lovely woman, but very confused, I think. She probably thought shagging me would make her happy because she'd have her revenge on her husband." He rubs the back of his neck, wincing faintly. "I assume that's why she told him we spent the night together. We didn't shag for the whole night, though. Just an hour or so, then we fell asleep. But she made it sound as if I fucked her like mad until morning. Still, I don't blame her. She has to live with that toerag."

I lean against him, though I'm not sure why. It feels right. "Did you enjoy having sex with a stranger?"

"No. It left a bad taste in my mouth." He lays his hand over mine on his arm. "I'm really not the way the tabloids have portrayed me. That's the Duke's version of events."

"Yeah, I know." He smells so good that I want to bury my face against his neck. But that would be so far beyond unprofessional that I'd have to fire myself for doing it. The soft, husky tone of his voice does strange things to me too. Maybe that explains why I say, "I have to admit, I'm curious about your reputation as Lord Steamy."

His gaze flicks to me, and his lips curl into a sexy smile. "How curious?"

"Very."

"If you really want to understand me..." He rotates toward me and cups my face in his hands. "You should experience Lord Steamy firsthand."

Yes, please, yes. That's what my body wants me to say. But my brain realizes this is a bad idea. I'll wind up with my face splashed across every tabloid. But he smells so good, and his eyes twinkle in the sunlight, and his hands feel warm and wonderful splayed across my cheeks. "I can't do that. It would be...um..."

"Wrong? Unprofessional?" He moves closer until his body brushes mine and his lips hover millimeters away. His breaths tease my mouth. "Isn't that what makes it exciting? We're alone in my flat. No one will ever know what we do here, together, right now."

His tone has become truly steamy, and my body reacts by growing slick and hot in all the best places.

Then he skims his lips over mine. "One kiss. Let me taste you, Avery, please."

"Oh, Hugh." I can't control my body anymore. It leans into him. While he tips my head back, I lay my palms on his chest and gaze into his eyes. "Kiss me."

Lord Steamy presses his mouth to mine.

I melt against him, closing my eyes so I can revel in the sensations of his soft lips exploring mine while he dives his fingers into my hair. The second he slips his tongue between my lips, I moan softly and surrender to the kiss. Gripping fistfuls of his shirt, I plunge my tongue into his mouth and moan again while I devour him like he's the most decadent dessert in the world and I'll never get to taste it again after this moment. He wraps his arms around me, hugging me to his hard body and the erection blossoming against my belly. I feel like I'm floating on a sensual cloud as he torments me with his tongue, coiling it around mine only to withdraw, then diving in again to tease the roof of my mouth.

One of his hands shifts down to my ass.

If he asked me to have sex with him right now, I'd say yes. We'd be halfway to heaven before I realized what I'd done. But this is only a kiss. Sure, it's the hottest, deepest, most incredible kiss in the history of the universe, and I want it to go on forever. Since I can't do that, I marshal every iota of willpower I have left, which isn't much, and pull my mouth away from his. He still holds me firmly against his body with his hand on my bottom. We're both breathing hard.

Holy shit. I never understood the Lord Steamy thing until just this minute. I'd treated it as a joke. But no, he genuinely does steam up a woman's libido. Can't blame the Duke's wife for screwing Hugh. I'd do it too if it weren't completely unethical.

Although I clear my throat, I can't summon the willpower to push him away. "Hugh, that was, um…"

"Now it's Hugh? What happened to 'I will only refer to you as Lord Sommerleigh'? You said that a few hours ago."

"I know. And I shouldn't have used your first name. Shouldn't have kissed you either." I wriggle free of his embrace and stagger backward a couple of steps. "This was a huge mistake. I'm sorry. I shouldn't have let that happen. From now on, we will only see each other at your office."

"There's no need to panic, darling. It was a kiss, not a binding contract for sex."

"But I work for your mother, and by extension, you. This is business, not a romantic dalliance. Nod your head if you understand and agree."

"I'm not a child, Avery. Yes, I understand. But I can't agree that this is nothing more than business, not after that kiss." He takes a step toward me, extending a hand, then seems to think better of it and shoves his hands into his pants pockets. "Would you like me to promise I'll behave myself?"

"You shouldn't make vows you can't keep. We both know flirting is like breathing to you. You said it yourself, it's a reflex."

He opens his mouth but shuts it again when I raise a hand.

"I will see you tomorrow at the office," I say. "Then we need to get started on removing that stain from your image."

"Better erase that blush from your cheeks too. It's a dead giveaway that someone kissed you thoroughly."

"Stop that. Uncontrolled flirtation is your downfall, remember? Besides, we will never kiss again. Strictly business." I walk toward the front door but stumble over my own feet. Great. That's exactly the wrong way to convince Hugh our kiss meant nothing. His soft chuckle spurs me to glare at him over my shoulder. "Good day, Lord Sommerleigh."

I hurry into the hall and pull the door shut.

Then it swings open again. "You forgot something, love."

When I whirl around, Hugh is standing there holding my purse. I snatch it from him. "Thank you."

I spin around again, marching off down the hallway. By the time I get into the elevator, I feel flustered again, like I had right after I peeled my mouth away from his. But I don't care how sexy that man is or how amazing that kiss was. Time to reassert my professional demeanor. Maybe I should quit this gig, since I can't swear I'll say no if he tries to seduce me, but I have never given up on a job. Quitting isn't in my nature.

That means I need to show Hugh Parrish how unaffected I am by what just happened. I still believe coming here had been the right thing to do for my client. Hugh relaxed more in his flat than he ever would have in the office, and I learned more about him. That information will help me do my job more effectively. But I will be in control now. Never again will Hugh Parrish hijack my work.

No, never again. Don't care that our kiss made me melt like he'd drizzled warm, molten caramel over my skin. I will never sleep with Hugh.

Chapter Five

Hugh

I've done it again, haven't I? Hugh Parrish has cocked things up and done exactly what everyone expects. I tried to seduce the wrong woman and nearly got myself into hot water again. And for what? One fucking incredible kiss. I shouldn't have done that, and now Avery hates me. Though I might not be the most perceptive man on earth, a fact that was demonstrated for me in excruciating fashion recently, I'm not an idiot. I know I made a mistake.

But I can't regret kissing Avery.

Grow up, you ruddy moron. Act like a CEO, not a randy teenager.

I need to do that, but I toss and turn all night while fantasizing about what Avery looks like naked. I liked the bossy image consultant in a designer skirt suit, but the jeans-wearing woman who walked into my flat and flirted with me... I like her the best. A woman in Avery's position must project a strong image. I understand that, but finding out she has a sexy softness underneath her professional exterior makes me hunger for more.

Of what? Another kiss? Or a shag?

I'm still debating what I really want when Avery Hahn bursts into my office with that leather portfolio in one hand. She closes the door, eying me with the same cool detachment I'd seen yesterday.

Wonderful. We're back to the working relationship in which she chastises me for…everything. I'm sure I'll be subjected to conversation along the lines of "Hugh is a bloody stupid arse." I suppress a sigh. Yes, I am a bloody stupid arse.

Avery sets her shapely bottom on the chair in front of my desk. "Good morning, Lord Sommerleigh."

I preferred the version of her who whispered "oh, Hugh" right before our lips met. Not likely to see that woman today. So I straighten my spine and smooth my suit jacket. "Good morning, Avery."

"You will call me Ms. Hahn."

"Of course." I roll my chair forward so I can fold my arms on the desktop. "Perhaps we should discuss yesterday. To clear the air."

"No need. That was a mistake. I should have known better than to fall for your Lord Steamy nonsense. It won't happen again." She flips her portfolio open and plucks up her pen. "Just to be clear, our relationship will remain strictly formal. I'm your image consultant. No more flirtation."

"Not sure I can control the impulse."

"Try harder."

Bloody hell, she's even tougher than yesterday. Our kiss must have affected her more deeply than she wants to admit. I can't deny that I love a strong, no-nonsense woman. Sometimes Avery reminds me of Kate Wagner. *Oh, fuck.* Is that why I'm attracted to Avery? Because she reminds me of the only woman who ever resisted my charms? Of course, Avery didn't resist, not yesterday.

I'll take her advice and try harder not to flirt. That's been my downfall, hasn't it? The fact that Avery reminds me of Kate proves I have a long way to go before I'm ready to be with any woman.

"We can at least be friends," I say. "That isn't off limits, is it?"

"Yesterday in this office, friendship was on the table." She crosses her legs, drawing my attention to her lovely knees. She snaps her fingers. "Wake up, Lord Sommerleigh."

"I was already awake."

"But you're still staring at my legs."

"Sorry." I jerk my attention back to her face. "I didn't mean to do that."

"Let me guess. It was a reflex."

The sarcasm dripping from her voice tells me everything I need to know. I haven't changed, and she will never trust me again—unless I can fix what I've bollocksed up. "I apologize for staring at your knees. From now on, I will behave."

"No, you won't." She slouches in her chair and shuts her eyes briefly. Then she shakes her head. "You really can't help yourself. I need to work around that, and you need to learn how to hide your libidinous tendencies. Polishing up your public image is my responsibility. But reforming a sex addict is beyond the scope of my job."

"Addict? You've got me wrong, darling."

"Every time you call me that, you prove my point."

I'm about to inform her how wrong she is when I realize what's really going on here. She loved that kiss as much as I did, and now she's panicking. Avery had done the same thing yesterday after we kissed. This morning, her panic has manifested as cool detachment.

Maybe I do have libidinous tendencies, but I've never kissed a woman who didn't want me to do that. Avery wanted it. She wanted me.

And now she thinks I'm a sex addict.

I lean back in my chair. "All right. Strictly business."

"Thank you." She pulls a newspaper out of her folder and tosses it onto my desk. "Take a look at that, Lord Sommerleigh. It's time you realized how serious your problem is."

"But I already know that."

"No, you don't." She nods toward the newspaper. "Look at the story at the bottom of the front page."

I unfold the newspaper and skim down to the story at the bottom: *Sommerleigh Sweets Poised for a Fall*. What in the world? That's rot. "I'm sure this is nothing but idle gossip."

"Oh really. Did you read the full article or just the headline? Because the article explains that your biggest distributor is on the verge of canceling your contract with them."

"This will blow over. These things always do."

Avery taps her fingernails on her portfolio. "You still don't grasp the scope of your problem. The Duke of Wackenbourne wants to destroy you, and he has the connections to do it. That article is the first salvo in a war that will ruin more than your reputation. It will wreck your family too."

"We Parrishes always land on our feet."

"Maybe you don't care about your company, but think about what this will do to your employees. If you lose your biggest distributor, they will lose their jobs."

Cold rushes through me as I realize the truth of what she said. I've considered only how my actions affected me, not what they might do to the people who depend on Sommerleigh Sweets for their livelihoods.

"It's one story," I say. "That doesn't mean—"

She jumps up and slaps her portfolio down on my desk. "Wake up, Lord Sommerleigh. The paper in your hand is the oldest and most respected financial newspaper in the UK, and one of the top five in the world. They don't report gossip."

My throat has grown tight, and swallowing doesn't help. I stare down at the newspaper, my gaze traveling up to the masthead. "This is today's edition?"

"Yes."

I scrub a hand over my mouth. "Blimey. I had no idea."

"Now that you do, maybe you'll follow my orders."

"Yes, of course. Whatever you say, I will do."

"Good." She sets her arse on the desk's edge. "Now that you understand the gravity of your situation, I have a radical suggestion."

"Radical?"

Memories of the last time someone used that word to describe my future barrel through my mind. The "radical intervention" crafted by the MacTaggart clan had changed my life, though not in an entirely good way. If Avery's idea is anything like that, I might as well move to a desert island and spend the rest of my life eating coconuts.

My mother's voice echoes in my mind. *Get your chin up, stiffen your upper lip, and stop behaving like a chancer.* Oh yes, my father would be ashamed of me. I haven't lived up to the title he bequeathed to me, and it's time I did.

I sit up straighter. "Tell me your idea, Ms. Hahn."

Her lips twitch at the corners, but she doesn't quite smile. "Are you sure you're fully committed to repairing your image and saving your company?"

"Yes. One hundred percent."

She sets her folder on the desk and clasps her hands on her thigh. "You need to get a girlfriend."

Laughter explodes out of me. "What? Shagging the wrong woman is what got me into this mess."

"I know. But you need the right kind of girlfriend to show the world you're not just a man-whore who screwed a duke's wife. The woman in your life should be respectable, mature, accomplished, fashionable, and attractive."

"Attractive? Looks don't matter. That's what women tell me."

"They're lying." Avery leans over my desk to plant one hand on the surface. "You don't need to find your soul mate. You need to convince the world that you've settled down and you're now a respectable viscount."

"How long will that take?"

"Normally, I allot at least two to three months to give a man an image makeover." She slants even closer. "But you don't have that much time. You need to get yourself into a stable relationship right away."

I stare at her. Has the woman gone insane? I can't find a girlfriend immediately, much less form a stable relationship with whatever woman I can talk into this bizarre scheme. A seed of an idea is taking root in my mind, though. A barmy idea, but desperate times call for reckless actions. Don't they?

While I consider my plan, I skim my gaze over Avery's body. Yes, she is attractive and fashionable, not to mention respectable, mature, and accomplished. The fact that I'd love to shag her has no bearing on my decision. If she wants me to get a girlfriend right now, she'll have to settle for my barmy idea.

I fold my arms on the desktop, my hands millimeters away from hers. "This would need to be a fake relationship. Yes? No one can find a serious girlfriend in an instant."

"That's right. But the fakeness needs to seem real."

"Of course." I glance at her thigh and the creamy skin exposed by the way she's leaning over my desk. "I know exactly how to fulfill your requirements."

"Good. Tell me your idea."

I rise and angle toward her, though not too much. If I mean to convince Avery, I need to channel the energy we'd shared yesterday in my flat. That means I need to become Lord Steamy, right here, right now, in my office with her. "The woman I have in mind is everything you mentioned in your list of requirements. I know she and I have chemistry, so pretending to be in love shouldn't be a problem."

"Another inappropriate sex partner won't do."

"But the person I know is not just another shag. She's a mature, accomplished, sexy, glamorous, powerful woman." I bend toward her until our faces hover a breath apart. "Her name is Avery Hahn."

Her face goes blank. She blinks once, slowly. Then she flattens her lips and blusters a breath out through her nostrils. "Honestly, sarcasm won't help. I was serious about you needing a respectable girlfriend."

"I was serious too. You are the only woman on earth who can both handle me and fulfill your requirements." I slide an arm around her waist and tug her into me. My lips graze hers as I speak. "That kiss yesterday proved you're the right woman for the job. Unless you're worried you can't resist me…"

"Of course I can."

"Then say yes to my plan. Be my instant fake relationship, Avery."

"Lord Sommerleigh—"

I flick my tongue out to tease her lips, rewarded by her quick intake of breath. "You wanted a radical solution. This is it."

For a moment, we sit here frozen in this position, our mouths almost touching and her chest heaving. Yes, Avery wants me. And I want her like mad. This plan will solve two problems at once—my need to kiss her again, and my need to save my company. At least, that's what I'm telling myself. Whether this will solve my problems or not remains an open question.

"Okay," Avery says. "Yes, I'll do it."

"Brilliant." I slide my hand down to her arse. "Now, how about our first kiss as a mature, respectable couple?"

"We don't need to show affection in private."

"Au contraire." I cradle her cheek in my free hand. "We need to keep up the pretense at all times, just in case anyone is spying on us."

"No, Lord Sommerleigh. You will never seduce me because I've inoculated myself against your charms. I'm immune now."

"Are you?" I paint a trail of light kisses across her cheek while I tip her head back in preparation for what we both want. "Let's test your theory."

I crush my lips to hers and hold that sexy body tightly against me while I dive my tongue deep into her mouth. She holds perfectly still and rigid—for about two seconds. Then I lash my tongue around hers, and she sags into me with the sweetest little moan I've ever heard.

And we ravish each other.

Chapter Six

Avery

What am I doing? I should not be kissing Hugh or diving my tongue into his mouth or throwing my arms around his neck. But in the past few seconds, I've done all three. We're consuming each other like the world might explode at any moment and we need to experience all the passion we possibly can before that happens.

This is crazy. I don't kiss my clients, and I certainly do not agree to become their fake girlfriend. Hugh Parrish has turned me into a lust-drunk lunatic. Resisting his advances shouldn't become the hardest thing I've ever had to do, but it is. Not that I've done much resisting.

God, I love the way he kisses. When he groans and squeezes my ass, I plunge my fingers into his hair and wriggle like I'm trying to climb onto him. Why does he have to taste so damn good? Feel so damn good? As hard as I've tried to convince myself I would never fall under Lord Steamy's spell again, I've done it anyway.

He peels his lips away from mine so slowly that my sex throbs. "How's that theory holding up?"

I blink rapidly and try to ignore the slickness between my thighs. "Huh? Oh, that. One kiss doesn't mean I've lost my immunity to you."

Lord Sommerleigh chuckles. "Doesn't it? My, you are stubborn. Fortunately, I like that in a woman."

"This will be a fake relationship. Remember that."

"Yes, I'll bear that in mind the next time you thrust your tongue into my mouth and try to mount me on my desk with your clothes on."

I slide off the desk and try to tug my jacket down, but I wind up stumbling sideways instead.

"Don't worry, darling," he says. "The effects of my charm wear off gradually. Sit down and let yourself recover."

"You are even more arrogant than I thought."

He sits down in his chair. "Maybe I am, but many women can attest to the power of my charms."

Why do I get the feeling I've accidentally reawakened the man-whore in him? Maybe I've just made a terrible mistake, but I can't back out now. If his reputation is shot, mine will be too. "This is a business arrangement, Lord Sommerleigh, not an excuse for hot sex. We will set parameters for this fake relationship."

"Go on. Tell me your parameters. What a sensual word that is."

Oh yeah, I've definitely reawakened Lord Steamy. *Good job, Avery.* "Pay attention, please. These are the rules. We will not kiss except in public and then only enough to convince everyone we're a genuine couple. Everything we do together will serve to promote the charade and convince the world we're in a serious relationship."

Hugh steeples his fingers, and his lips curve into a sly, sexy expression. "A couple in a serious relationship would be shagging."

"No sex. You will not touch me in any intimate way unless it's part of the aforementioned public displays."

"I love the way you say 'aforementioned.' It makes me want to kiss you again."

"Too bad. Kissing is off limits except—"

"In public. Yes, yes, I heard your ruddy rules." He rises and offers me his hand. "Let's formally seal our pretense. I vow I shall not seduce you unless you want me to do it. It's your turn."

I slip my hand into his. "We have a deal."

"You didn't vow not to seduce me. That's probably best, since you can't keep your lips off me."

We shake hands, and I pull mine away. "No flirting, Lord Sommerleigh."

"That wasn't part of our agreement. We already shook on it, so we can't add another parameter."

Oh, the sneaky Brit. He left himself a little loophole that gives him an excuse to flirt with me. Well, I can resist that. I'm a professional, and I will stick to my job.

A memory flashes in my mind—Hugh in nothing but a towel, until he dropped it and gave me a full-frontal view of his nude body.

Damn. Why did I think of that?

"How will this work?" he asks. "We should be seen in public, naturally. But since I need that image repair to happen quickly, how do we fabricate a relationship without it seeming forced?"

"You went to Scotland recently. We can say we met there. I was working with a client, and you were visiting your best friend. We clicked, and things took off from there."

"But I shagged Annabelle after Scotland."

Shoot, I forgot about that. "Okay, we can say we met there and became friends. But we didn't realize how we felt about each other until later."

"Why would anyone believe a clever, accomplished woman like you would want to date a man who fucked a duke's wife in between meeting and falling for you?" He sinks into his chair, his posture slumping. "This won't work. We need more time to build up the farce."

He makes a good point. I would've realized how hard this would be if I weren't still recovering from our kiss. Maybe we don't need a convoluted explanation. Maybe all we need is Hugh.

"You're right," I say. "We do need more time. And there's an obvious solution to that problem."

"What sort of solution?"

I point a finger at him. "You, Lord Sommerleigh. Marshal all your charm and intelligence to convince that distributor to stick with you for a while longer. Come on, you can do it." I lean forward to pat his cheek. "Seduce them into staying. We both know you excel at that."

"Seducing women is my forte. I can't use my Lord Steamy techniques on a company."

"You're creative and smart, and I know you can come up with something. Seduce them, Hugh. It's your only shot at salvation."

He gazes down at his lap for several seconds. When he lifts his gaze to me, I swear I can see a sneaky glint in his eyes. "Will you help me practice my speech? The one designed to seduce a distributor into staying in bed with me."

If he thinks that saying "seduce" and "in bed" in the same sentence will brainwash me into having sex with him... Well, I can't swear it won't work. But I will summon all my willpower to avoid letting that happen.

"Yes, I'll help you," I say. "But we need to get started on fabricating a relationship too. That means going on a date."

"Where and when?"

"Tonight. You choose the venue. But make it someplace where people you know will see us together."

He grunts. "Everyone in the country knows me now, thanks to the Duke of sodding Wackenbourne."

"We can use that to our advantage. Choose a romantic restaurant and make a reservation."

"I doubt I can get a reservation at an appropriate venue for tonight. Everyone will expect me to take you to a renowned restaurant."

"Charm your way into a reservation."

He rolls his eyes. "You overestimate my power over others. Women I can handle. But a maître d'? Not sure I can manage that."

This man confuses the heck out of me. One minute, he's arrogantly certain of himself, the next he's vulnerable and unsure. I wonder if he was always this way, or if his mysterious time in Scotland changed him. I'll have plenty of time to plumb the depths of Hugh Parrish while we fake date.

"You can manage it," I tell him. "Believe in yourself. That's the only way we can save your reputation."

"All right." He grabs his cell phone. "Whilst I wait for a miracle to occur, I'll charm a maître d' into giving us a last-minute reservation."

"Good. You can do it, I know you can."

He stares at me without blinking for just long enough that I'm about to ask what's wrong. Then he makes a strange face and dials his phone.

And I listen while Lord Steamy unleashes his considerable charm on a restaurant employee. Despite his cheerful tone, his expression stays slightly pinched. Within a minute at most, he thanks whoever he'd been talking to and ends the call, setting his phone on the desktop.

He gives me a tight smile. "I've booked us a table for eight o'clock this evening. Wear a sexy frock, preferably designer. No one will believe I would go out with a woman in a business suit. Though I happen to love the way you look in professional clothes—or in jeans and a loose-fitting blouse."

"Thank you." I back away and sit down on the chair across from him. "You can pick me up at my hotel, at the door to my room. That's what two people going on a date would do."

"Of course."

I glance around, searching for where I left my portfolio.

"Looking for this?" Hugh says. "You left it on my desk."

He deftly tosses the portfolio to me.

I catch it and flip the leather folder open, grabbing my pen from inside it. "Now, we need to discuss how you will behave, both on our date and in everyday life. You should be mindful of your body language and try to maintain a relaxed demeanor."

"As if that's so bloody easy."

"Let's practice."

"In what way?"

"Take me on a tour of Sommerleigh Sweets."

He twists his mouth into an expression I've already figured out means he doesn't want to follow my orders, but he'll do it anyway. "We're in the corporate offices. The factory is ten miles away."

"Take me there, please."

Hugh studies me with his eyes squinted. "Does anyone know you're my image consultant? Other than Mum, I mean."

"No. I wouldn't be a trusted consultant if I blabbed to everyone about who I'm working for and why."

"What about Trudy?"

"She doesn't know either. I didn't make an appointment. I ambushed you—on purpose. Knocking you off balance helped kick off the process."

"I see." Hugh sits there staring at me for a few seconds, then he pushes his chair back and stands. "All right. If you insist on getting the grand tour, we'll need some sort of explanation of who you are and why you're here." He bows his head and groans. "This won't work. Unless you mean to use an alias, everyone will know what you do for a living."

"No, they won't. Confidentiality is key in my business." I pull out a business card and stand up to hand it to him. "Look at this. My card includes my name and contact information, but under my name it says only 'consultant.' I do that on purpose. No one wants their maid or their grandmother to know I'm fixing a problem for them."

"How do you get clients, then? 'Consultant' is awfully vague."

"Clients come to me thanks to word of mouth."

"You mean one bloke you helped out of trouble told his mate about you when that bloke needed help."

"Essentially."

He walks out from behind his desk and offers me his arm. "Shall we take my car to the factory?"

"Yes. And we can tell everyone I'm a business consultant."

"Sounds reasonable."

I glance at his arm that he still holds in a bent and slightly raised position, as if he wants me to hook mine around it. "This is business, Lord Sommerleigh. We haven't known each other long enough, in reality or in our fake relationship, for me to accept your chivalrous gesture."

A sigh gusts out of him, and he lowers his arm. "I'll be a good little boy and pretend we haven't kissed passionately twice."

He didn't say that in his Lord Steamy voice. I think he's genuinely disappointed that I wouldn't take his arm. Does Hugh have a gentlemanly side? That doesn't jibe with what I know about him, but then, I don't know that much. Mostly what I read in tabloids. His mother had been reluctant to offer details, which I understood. Lady Sommerleigh might be paying me, but Hugh is my client.

I grab my purse, and Hugh opens the door for me. I thank him with a nod of acknowledgment. He informs Trudy that he's taking me out to the factory but that first we will stop in at the vice president's office down the hall to introduce Sommerleigh Sweets' new business consultant.

The farce has begun.

Hugh leads me down the hall to a doorway marked with a plaque that identifies the occupant as "Rupert Parrish, Vice President." After two crisp knocks, Hugh ushers me into the office.

A man with salt-and-pepper hair sits behind a desk in front of a big window. He doesn't have a corner office, like the CEO. The man glances up at us and smiles. "Hugh, what a lovely surprise. I'd heard you might not come in today."

"Who told you that? I never said anything of the sort."

"Ah, well, I think it was more of a rumor." The man fusses with his tie and glances at me, then looks at Hugh. "Who is your guest?"

"This is Avery Hahn. She's a business consultant who has graciously agreed to help us through this difficult time. Avery, meet my cousin Rupert. I couldn't run this company without him."

I shake hands with Rupert. "Are you a viscount or something too?"

"Afraid not. I'm just a normal bloke."

"But you're instrumental in running this company. That means you're not just a normal guy. Don't be so modest."

Rupert fusses with his tie again while staring down at his shirt. "Well, Hugh is the CEO."

Have I embarrassed him? I didn't mean to, but it seems like I did.

"Now that you two have met," Hugh says, "it's time for that tour of the factory. Would you care to join us, Rupert?"

"Sorry. I'm driving Lizzie to school. It's her first day at Oxford, you know."

"Of course. Well then, Avery and I will be off."

We exit his cousin's office and board an elevator. Hugh's office is on the top floor of a ten-story building that houses the offices of various other companies too. I briefly worry that he might try to kiss me again, but he behaves like a true gentleman.

Am I a little disappointed? Maybe. But I will never admit that to Hugh.

Chapter Seven

Hugh

A factory tour must be the most boring activity I have ever undertaken as CEO of Sommerleigh Sweets. Honestly, I haven't visited the factory often. Once or twice a year at most. As CEO, I'm not expected to go there. I often wonder if I should have more of a presence, but I always feel like I'd be in the way if I tried to cultivate a more hands-on style.

It's a factory. I know nothing about that rubbish.

But I convince the foreman, Len Jones, to give us the grand tour. He seems rather surprised when I suggest it because tours are for, well, tourists. I try not to flinch when Len announces loudly that Lord Sommerleigh has come for a visit. I wondered why he made us wait in his office while he "got things ready" for me and Avery. Now I know.

He instructed all the employees to line up in two rows, all the better for me to prance down the aisle between them like a sodding royal. I'm a viscount, not a prince. For pity's sake, this is overkill.

I do my bit, though. I smile and shake everyone's hand and tell them how much I appreciate their hard work. That's not a load of pig's wallow. I do appreciate it. These working-class folk toil away so my family can get richer. Yet now my behavior has put all their livelihoods at risk. Everything I do from this moment on must serve to rescue my company so the people who work for me won't lose their sole source of income.

Every time I feel like whingeing about my life, I should remember these people.

After the tour, I drop Avery off at her hotel. Mum has set her up at one of the most expensive hotels in London. Well, Avery deserves the best. She agreed to become my fake girlfriend to improve my chances of convincing the world I'm not a bloody stupid arse who accidentally slept with the Duchess of Wackenbourne. I shagged her on purpose, but I had no idea who she was.

When I get back to the office, I fight the unconscious impulse to ask Trudy to ring the bloke in charge of Jenkins Foods, our largest distributor. I need to do this myself, from start to finish. So I ask Trudy for the number, which causes her to stare at me as if I've asked my executive assistant to show me her knickers. I don't normally handle calls in this manner, so I can't blame her for being surprised.

She jots down the number and hands me the slip of paper.

I thank her and hurry into my office, shutting the door to ensure Trudy won't hear it if I cock this up. I've just sat down when my mobile rings. The caller ID tells me who it is, and I can't help groaning.

Because it says, "Callum MacTaggart."

My best mate wants to talk to me. I can guess why, but I've avoided speaking to him ever since I came home from Scotland. It's childish, I know. Rather than behaving like a coward, I need to start removing the tarnish from my reputation by acting like an adult.

Still, I wait through two more rings before I answer. "Hello, Callum."

Do I say that in a tone reminiscent of a man about to be hung from the gallows? Possibly.

"What's fashing you?" Callum asks. "Do ye know how many times I've rung you but only got your voice mail?"

I can hear the concern in his voice, and it triggers an itch under my skin. "Nothing is 'fashing' me. I'm feeling wonderful today."

"Like hell you are. I know ye too well to believe that."

Bollocks. I can't even lie convincingly to Callum. How will I pull off a fake relationship with Avery? Oh, the answer isn't that hard to figure out. I'll be much more convincing with Avery because I want to shag her.

"I'm sorry, Callum," I say. "Things have been...difficult lately. Up there in the Highlands, you probably haven't seen the tabloids."

"Oh aye, we've seen the stories about you. We have the internet, ye know."

How did I not see that coming? The sodding internet goes everywhere.

"Is it true?" Callum asks. "Did ye shag a duchess?"

"Yes, unfortunately, that is true. I didn't know who she was, but I shouldn't have gotten a leg over with a stranger. It was a stupid, selfish thing to do." I rest my forehead in my palm and groan. "Now my company might be ruined as thoroughly as I am."

"Relax, Hugh, it'll pass. Tough times always do."

"You sang a different tune back when your brother sent you to physical therapy."

"But he did the right thing. I'm grateful to Jack because I would never have met Kate otherwise."

Ah, the lovely Kate. She claimed she wanted nothing to do with romance, but that only applied to me. Now Callum and Kate are planning their nuptials.

"Will ye come to the wedding?" my best mate asks. "Ye missed the engagement ceilidh, but I know you're busy. It's a lot to ask—"

"Of course I'll be there. It's not too much to ask." I've given him that impression, though, by refusing to answer his calls. He must think... Well, it hardly matters now. "I'll be there, Callum."

"It's in three weeks." He pauses. "Are you sure ye want to come?"

"Yes, I'm sure."

"Well, ah, in that case..." He pauses again, for longer this time. "No, I cannae ask that."

I stifle another groan because I have a feeling I know what he wants to ask me. I'd love to say absolutely no, but I was there when he fell for Kate. I know she changed his life, and I understand what that means to him. I can't say no. "The answer is yes, Callum, I will be your best man."

"Really? That's brilliant, Hugh."

"Yes, I'm excited too." But I sound like a condemned man again. "See you in three weeks."

"Donnae let your scandal get to you. Everything will work out. Bring a lass with ye to the wedding, even if she's not your soul mate. Get out there again."

Not long ago, my best mate had turned into a grumpy sod who snapped at everyone. Thanks to Kate, he's the old Callum again. And now I'm the grumpy sod who's fucked up his own life.

Callum and I say goodbye. It's time for me to bite that bullet and see if I can chew it into smaller pieces. So I ring Phillip Jenkins.

His executive assistant answers. "Jenkins Foods, Megan speaking. How may I assist you?"

"I need to speak to Mr. Jenkins, please," I say. "This is Hugh Parrish, the Viscount Sommerleigh, of Sommerleigh Sweets."

Ever since I became a viscount, my mother has drummed it into my head that I must assert my title whenever it's appropriate, especially in business. I feel like a ruddy fool every time I heed her command.

"Oh, Lord Sommerleigh," the woman says with no small measure of anxiety evident in her voice. "I'm afraid—It's just that—Hold, please."

Jenkins doesn't want to talk to me. He must've instructed his executive assistant to refuse my calls.

No, I'm being paranoid.

"Lord Sommerleigh?" Megan says when she finally comes back on the line. "I'm afraid Mr. Jenkins just left for an important meeting. He won't be back today, but he says he'll contact you as soon as he has time in his schedule."

Wonderful. That means I'll need to take Avery's advice and try to charm this woman into letting me speak to Jenkins. "Can't you squeeze me in, darling? It's rather urgent, and I would be very grateful for your help. Perhaps I could meet Mr. Jenkins for lunch."

"He'll be out all day." She hesitates yet again. "I really am sorry, Lord Sommerleigh. I love your sweets, especially the caramel-filled ones."

Am I being granted a slender thread of hope? Maybe I'm just desperate because I hear myself saying, in that blasted Lord Steamy voice, "Why don't I send you a package of our silkiest, most decadent dark-chocolate caramel truffles? The silky centers will melt on your tongue like sin itself."

"I'm not supposed to accept gifts at work."

But I can tell from her tone that she wants to accept that silky, decadent gift from me. "Why don't I send the package to your home, darling? It's a thank-you for all your help."

"I don't know..."

"You'll never taste anything more luscious than Sommerleigh truffles."

"All right. You can send them to my home." Megan rattles off her address while I write it down. "This is very kind of you, Lord Sommerleigh."

"Not at all. Goodbye, darling."

She giggles. "Goodbye."

I didn't get to speak to Phillip Jenkins, but I've made an ally at his company. Sweet-talking a man's executive assistant is a stepping-stone, one I admit I've employed before. Doing this never used to bother me, but these days, it does.

Only a little bit.

Well, possibly more than a bit.

Though I want to go home and hide, I force myself to stay at work all day. I've never behaved like such a ruddy coward, but lately, I feel like an impostor and keep waiting for the real Lord Sommerleigh to walk into the room and toss me out on my arse. Not that long ago, I was confident and ready for anything. Now, I slump behind my desk, desperately struggling to pay attention to the documents I'm meant to read and understand.

But the words blur together.

Everything I need to get done today takes three times longer than it should—until two forty-five p.m. That's when my mobile rings. I don't even glance at the caller ID, but simply answer with a half-mumbled hello.

"What color suit will you be wearing tonight, Lord Sommerleigh?"

Avery's voice makes me jerk upright, no longer slumping in my chair, and my pulse accelerates. "Pardon?"

"I said what color suit will you wear."

Since I hadn't even thought about that yet, I decide to have a little fun with her. "Are you trying to initiate phone sex with me? Whenever women ask that question, sex is what they have in mind. So tell me, what are you wearing, darling?"

"What are you wearing *tonight* is what I asked. Don't get ahead of yourself, Lord Sommerleigh."

"If you don't mean to phone-shag me, why are you speaking in a sultry voice?"

"Didn't mean to."

"But you're still doing it, love." I hook one ankle over the other knee and begin to rock my chair gently. "You have the sexiest voice I've ever heard. Say something naughty, darling, please."

"We're not having phone sex, Hugh."

"Ah, but you just called me by my first name. You only do that when you want me."

Silence. But I can tell she's still on the line.

My cock is getting stiffer by the second.

"Do you phone-shag a lot of women?" she asks, her voice even sultrier.

"I wouldn't say a lot, but I do enjoy whispering naughty things to a woman while listening to her come."

"Mm-hm, I can picture you doing that." A rustling sound follows. "I'm lying on the sofa. Are you in your office?"

She's going to do it. All-business Avery wants to phone-shag with me.

My cock is straining my trousers.

"Yes, darling," I say. "I'm in my office, relaxing in my chair. Would you like me to tell you what to do?"

"Oh, yes. Please."

"What are you wearing?"

"Jeans and a T-shirt."

I close my eyes and imagine her lying on a sofa, dressed the way she described. "Unzip your jeans, love."

A pause. "I unzipped them."

"Slide your hand inside your knickers and tell me how wet you are."

I am having phone sex with Avery. Can't believe it. But there is no way on earth I'll stop now.

"Oh God," she says, her voice a husky whisper. "I'm so wet my fingers are covered in my cream, and all the hairs down there are soaked. So are my panties."

Bloody hell. My breaths grow shorter and sharper, and my cock throbs while I envision Avery touching herself. I undo my trousers and shove a hand inside to palm my erection. My voice grows rougher as I tell her, "Stroke your fingers up and down your folds. And tell me how much you wish I were there fucking you."

"Oh, Hugh, I want you inside me right now."

I hear more rustling, as if she's writhing on that sofa while she strokes herself. Her breaths quicken, becoming soft little gasps.

"Stop," I tell her. The sound of her movements ceases, and I have no doubt she heeded my command. "Rub your clit for me. Do it now."

Yes, I've done phone sex before. But I have never commanded a woman to do what I say while we get our ends away. No, I whisper and tease my lovers. But with Avery, I need to order her to do my bidding.

She moans.

"Are you rubbing?" I ask.

"Mm, yes."

I love the hungry tone in her voice. That alone makes me so fucking randy that I start to pump my cock. "Keep rubbing that nub, love, and pet your flesh with your longest finger at the same time. Drag it up and down, up and down. I'm going to stroke my-self while you do that."

"Hugh, I—Oh shit, I'm already so close."

"I know, love, I know." Can hardly breathe now, and the rapid pace of her gasps assures me she is on the edge. I can push her over it so easily. "Close your eyes, picture me fucking you, and come for me, Avery."

Her sharp cry dissolves into whimpering and gradually fades into silence.

I pump myself several more times and swallow a shout as I come.

"Hugh, that was...wow."

Though I'm breathing so hard my ears are ringing, I manage to speak. "Yes, love, that was wow."

For a moment, neither of us says anything.

Then Avery sighs with deep contentment. "So, are you going to tell me what you'll be wearing tonight? I'd like us to be color-coordinated."

"What?" I still haven't caught my breath, and she's moved on to what clothing we should wear for our date. "No bloody idea. Does it matter?"

"Choose a grey suit. It'll look hot on you and go with anything I wear. Maybe I'll surprise you with my dress."

"Yes, fine, whatever." I understood the words grey suit and dress, but nothing else.

"Remember to pick me up at eight. I'm in Room 440. Goodbye, Lord Sommerleigh."

She disconnects the call.

And I lie here slumped in my chair trying to remember what words are and why I need them. Doesn't matter.

Because Avery Hahn just stole my sanity.

Chapter Eight

Avery

I stand in front of the full-length mirror in my hotel suite and examine my outfit to make sure I haven't forgotten anything. Am I nervous about my date with Hugh? No, I think I'm excited. After what we did this afternoon, I expected to feel weird about seeing him again. The flutter in my tummy every time I think about Lord Sommerleigh might be a warning sign, but I don't care.

Heaven help me, I had phone sex with Hugh Parrish—and I loved it. I've never done anything like that before. If I want to get off by myself, I don't need a man to call and tell me how to do it. But I loved listening to Hugh's rough, hungry voice while he ordered me to touch myself.

As hot as that was, I want more. I want real sex. With him.

I can't do it. I know that. We agreed to a fake relationship for public viewing only, and we agreed to keep it professional the rest of the time. Okay, then why did I agree to phone sex? Hugh spoke in his Lord Steamy voice, and I lost every last shred of my common sense.

Yes, it's his fault.

What would sex with Hugh be like? Steamy and sensual. Vigorous and breath-taking. Slow and intimate. Hot and hard and incredible. I think it would be all those things and more, but I cannot ever get hot and dirty with him again. Is this the third time I've caved and let him do things to me that are totally inappropriate? I've lost count.

Someone knocks on the door to my suite.

My pulse throbs faster, and suddenly, I have trouble taking a full breath. Oh no, I *am* excited to see Hugh again. Really excited. But I can and will maintain the proper decorum. No going down on him under the table in the restaurant. To distract myself from that thought, I take another look at myself in the mirror. My deep-purple dress brings out the lavender shades in my eyes, and the backless design makes me feel sexy even while the neckline reveals only the barest hints of my cleavage. The long skirt falls just at my ankles, and my stiletto heels match the dress.

I force myself to walk out of the bedroom and across the living room instead of sprinting. Then I pull the front door open and give Hugh a calm smile. "Good evening, Lord Sommerleigh."

"Good evening, Avery." He rakes his gaze over me. "You look good enough to devour, darling. And you should call me Hugh, don't you think? We are pretending to date, after all."

"Of course. You're right, Hugh."

He skims his gaze over me again while rubbing his jaw. "Avery, you are the most beautiful and desirable woman I have ever laid eyes on."

"Thank you. I love your gray suit. It's elegant and sexy." And that suit makes me want to drag him over to the sofa and say to hell with dinner. But I restrain my lust. Barely.

He offers me his arm. "Shall we go, darling?"

"Yes." I curl my arm around his. "Where are we going?"

"To the sort of place where everyone shows up in designer clothes and no one asks how much anything costs."

"So we're showing all those rich snobs that you aren't a total sleaze. You are a gentleman."

"Precisely." He leads me out the door and pulls it shut, then looks at me. "Are you sure you want to do this? Once everyone sees us together, there will be no stopping the gossip train."

"I'm sure."

He seems almost puzzled, but he guides me toward the elevator without saying anything else. We ride in a car with three other people, so I can't ask him what's wrong. By the time we climb into a limo, I've forgotten what I wanted to ask him.

I get into the car first and sit on one of two bench seats that face each other. I expect Hugh to sit beside me, but instead, he settles onto the opposite bench and stretches an arm across its back. A solid partition separates us from the driver.

"Shouldn't you sit over here?" I ask. "We're supposed to be a couple, you know."

"Yes, I'm aware of that." He winces and scratches the back of his neck. "I feel a bit odd about it all of a sudden, like I'm seducing you into becoming my mistress."

"I agreed to this arrangement. Do you think you're so hot that I can't say no to anything you suggest?"

He almost smirks but can't quite do it when he's still grimacing slightly. "I did seduce you into phone sex."

"You suggested it. I agreed. That's not seduction." I wish we weren't talking about our phone-shag incident because it's making me wet and achy. I want to change the subject, but I need an answer to my question. "Why won't you sit over here with me?"

He flattens his lips, drumming his fingers on his seat. Then he jumps over to my side, though he keeps an arm's length between us. "Happy now?"

"Not quite." I shimmy sideways until my thigh brushes against his. "That's better."

Maybe I like being close to him a little too much. No point in worrying about that now. I need to mentally prepare myself for our fake date.

Hugh slides an arm across my shoulders. "I hope I haven't corrupted you with my craven lust."

"Craven? I assume you're talking about our phone-sex incident. That was hot, and I loved it, end of story." I lay a hand on his thigh, not realizing I've done that until he stiffens and stares at me. "I'm the one who kissed you twice, remember?"

"No, you asked *me* to kiss *you* the first time."

"I instigated it, which is the same as doing it myself. But that's not the point. You shouldn't feel like a criminal for what we did on the phone. I'm a big girl, and I make my own decisions."

"Of course. But—"

I seal his lips with two of my fingers. "No buts. It was amazing, period."

He smiles against my fingers, then peels them away from his mouth. "Have it your way, darling. I'm helpless to deny a woman anything she wants."

When our car pulls up in front of the restaurant, we wait for the driver to get out and open the door for us. Hugh swears that's what proper aristocrats do. He'd rather open the door himself, he tells me, but he needs to behave like a viscount if he's serious about repairing his image.

I congratulate him on committing to the process at last.

And he kisses my cheek, right before he climbs out and offers me his hand to help me step out of the limo. I know he's not faking it. He truly is a gentleman—with a steamy, dirty alter ego.

He keeps a hand on my back while we ascend the steps that lead into the restaurant. Paparazzi snap pictures of us. I knew that would happen, and it's what we need to happen. Being seen in public as a respectable viscount with a respectable date on his arm is the best way to convince everyone he's not a bastard.

At the top of the steps, Hugh offers me his arm, and I take it.

Within thirty seconds of entering the restaurant, we sit down at a table in the middle of everything, exactly where we need to be. Hiding in a corner booth won't show the London snobs that Hugh is a gentleman. He needs to be seen, and that means eating in full view of all the patrons.

Hugh puts on a brave face, but I can tell by his minute facial tics that he's not entirely comfortable being on display for everyone to judge. He rests a hand on the table, which might seem like a casual, relaxed gesture to anyone else. But I've spent time with Hugh, in his office and his flat, and I learned some of his mannerisms. I'll need to learn a lot more if we're going to pull this off.

After the waiter sets water glasses on our table and hands us menus, I lean forward to lay a palm on Hugh's hand. "Relax, you're doing great."

"I appreciate the encouragement, but I think my best course of action is to ignore everyone. Unless someone speaks to me or waves at me."

"Okay. Let's order and then have a nice chat. That's appropriate dating behavior."

"Good. I can do that. I think."

"Yes, you can do it."

Ten minutes later, after ordering our food, it's time to start the conversation. Okay, I really, really want to ask him about Scotland. But I won't do that. He got upset when I broached the subject in his apartment, and I need him relaxed tonight. So I opt for a safer topic. "Are you close with your cousin Rupert? I know you don't have any siblings, because your mother told me that, but she didn't mention other relatives."

"I have several cousins who are like siblings to me. Rupert is the oldest and the only one who works with me at Sommerleigh Sweets."

"He seems like a nice guy."

"Yes, he is a good bloke. He and his wife had a scare a few months ago when it seemed like she might have cancer, but it turned out to be nothing. I volunteered to mind their two young daughters for three days so they could concentrate on the medical issues."

"You babysat kids? In your swanky flat?"

He shakes his head. "I went home to Sommerleigh and spent those three days with my mother and the girls."

"You are an amazing man. Not many single guys would do that for a cousin."

"Since I don't have brothers or sisters, my cousins have become surrogate siblings. We see each other whenever I go home, though I prefer to stay in London."

I eat some of my food, giving Hugh a chance to do the same before I ask another question. "Isn't your best friend like a brother to you?"

"Yes, of course. Callum is the closest I have to a brother, though I've let our relationship founder a bit lately."

Callum is his Scottish best friend. I want to discuss that topic more, but it's part of the clearly painful events that happened in Scotland. I'll save that talk for another time. "You can ask me a question, you know."

"Are you sure you want me prying into your personal life?"

"Yes. That's part of dating. We need to learn more about each other in case anyone asks us questions. If we don't know at least the basics, it will be obvious we're not a genuine couple."

"I see." Hugh taps his fork on his plate's rim while he studies me. "What about your family? Your parents?"

"Mom died in a car accident when I was twelve. Dad passed away during my sophomore year at college. He had an aneurysm."

"I'm so sorry. My father died when I was at university too. It was a heart attack. That's when I became the Viscount Sommerleigh."

We have something in common that I never would've expected—loss.

Hugh still holds his fork, though he's stopped tapping it. "Do you have any siblings?"

"I have a brother, Derek. He's three years older than I am."

"Do you get on?"

"Mm-hm. He's a great guy, but he can be a little overprotective at times."

"Of course he's overprotective. You're a beautiful woman and must have all sorts of lustful blokes clamoring to seduce you." His lips curl into a sly smile, and his eyes sparkle with humor. "I'm one of those blokes."

"Don't think I'll tell Derek about Lord Steamy. He'd fly over here just to punch your lights out, then he'd drag me back to America."

"I'm not afraid of a rollicking fight. I've battled angry Scots, after all."

"You have? When?" I hadn't intended to ask about Scotland. But he mentioned it, and the question popped out of my mouth. "I know you don't want to talk about that yet. I didn't think before I spoke."

"Everyone does that occasionally. I'm not annoyed that you asked. But no, I don't want to discuss it."

"I hope sometime you will tell me about that."

He stares down at his plate and pokes at the remnants of his meal. "Maybe later. Much later."

"Okay." I take a sip of the chardonnay Hugh had ordered for us. It's delicious, but I'm drinking it right now only because I need time to think about what to say next to lighten the mood. "Would you like to know anything else about me?"

His head pops up, and that sly smile returns. "Oh yes, darling. I'd love to know every last thing about you."

"That's a tall order. I'd need more than one evening to share everything with you."

"Let's start with mundane things. Music, films, et cetera."

I grin. "Never heard anyone use the term et cetera in casual conversation before."

"Then you haven't met the right sort of man." He picks up his wine glass and swirls the liquid inside it while peering at me over the glass's rim. "A proper gentleman knows how important language is to seduction."

I'm getting tingly just listening to him. The words he spoke don't do that to me. Well, it's not only the words. The way he speaks them in that sensual, soft, deliciously British voice lights a spark inside me. Hugh knows how to stoke the flames until I'm burning for him like a wildfire.

He tips the wine glass toward his lips in slow motion, letting the golden liquid slide between his lips. "You know what I mean, Avery. I demonstrated the principle for you this afternoon."

Phone sex. That's what he means. And naturally, he employed his Lord Steamy voice when he spoke those words. The tingling between my thighs has transformed into molten slickness.

I need to calm this down immediately, before he talks me into sneaking into the bathroom for an erotic interlude. "We shouldn't talk about that. If you want to prove to everyone that you're not a calculating womanizer, better stop thinking what I know you're thinking right now."

"But we're dating. The standard ritual does involve sex."

Crossing my legs in a vain hope I can squelch the fire he ignited on purpose, I push my plate away. "Time to take me home, Hugh."

That smile widens into a wicked grin. "Anything you want, darling."

Chapter Nine

Hugh

I meant it's time for you to drop me off at my hotel," Avery says. Her lips curl up in a sweet little half smile that dimples her cheeks. "You know that's what I meant. But you honestly can't help yourself, can you? Flirtation flows out of you like water."

"Steaming hot water, naturally." Sighing, I push my chair back. "But I will take you home if you insist on denying us both the pleasure of...well, pleasure. As a proper gentleman, I should see you to the door of your suite."

Avery shakes her head. "Hugh…"

"I love the way you turn a single syllable into a reprimand." I wave to the waiter. While he wends his way around the other tables, heading toward us, I tell Avery, "Should I have you sign a waiver stating that I did not seduce you because you in fact begged me to—"

"Shush, Hugh. The waiter is almost within earshot. And so are the people at nearby tables."

"Then I'll speak in a softer voice. I know you love that."

"If you mean the you-know-what voice, it won't work this time."

"Won't it?"

The waiter reaches us and hands me the bill. Avery watches me give him my credit card, and the bloke discreetly scurries away. She keeps watching while I bring out several pound notes and select the right amount for the waiter's tip.

"You could've added that to the bill," she says, "instead of laying cash on the table."

"I prefer to leave tips in cash. If I add it to the credit card payment, the server won't get the money until much later."

"Really? I never thought of that."

"Most people don't. Credit cards are more convenient, but cash is better for the person receiving the tip."

She tilts her head to the side, regarding me with a slightly surprised expression. "You genuinely are a nice guy—a true gentleman."

"Does that surprise you?"

"Yes, but not because of your reputation. Most men aren't as considerate and sweet as you."

"Thank you, love. I appreciate the compliment."

Once I've signed the credit card slip for the waiter, I hurry over to Avery's chair so I can pull it out for her before she does it herself. I'm a considerate and sweet gentleman, after all. She's not the first woman to say something like that to me, but she is the first one to make me feel oddly invigorated by the compliment.

A few minutes later, we're sliding onto the bench seat in the limousine, side by side. I drape an arm across the seat behind her head, and she rests her cheek on my shoulder. I resist my every impulse to say something naughty, which means I don't suggest we shag in the limo, or in the elevator of her hotel, or inside her suite. No, I do something far more shocking.

I kiss her good night, on the cheek, at the door to her suite, and wait until she shuts the door behind her. Then I walk away.

None of the women I'd known before Avery would've wanted me to leave without shagging them. They would have been insulted if I hadn't even tried to smooth-talk my way into their boudoir. But with this woman, I don't want to rush into full-on sex. I want to take my time and get to know her. Does that mean we're legitimately dating?

I get my answer the next day when Avery shows up at my office—carrying her leather portfolio, of course.

She settles her lovely arse onto the chair across from my desk. "Good morning, Lord Sommerleigh."

"I thought we agreed you should call me Hugh, since we're dating."

"Fake dating. Besides, at work, I should still call you by your title." She crosses her legs and bounces the toe of her dangling shoe as if she's tapping it on the floor. "Have you spoken to that distributor yet?"

"No. Well, I spoke to Phillip Jenkins's executive assistant, Megan, but she claimed he was unavailable."

"Didn't you try laying on the charm?"

"Yes. That girl now has a crush on me, but I still can't speak to Jenkins."

Her foot-bouncing stops. She loosely puckers her lips but says nothing for a moment that seems to drag on forever. Whenever she scrutinizes me that way, I feel like a little boy who's about to get scolded by his nanny—a sexy as hell one, for sure.

"Stop that," she says. "Stop it right now."

"What? I haven't done anything."

"You were thinking about sex." She leans forward. "We're at work, which means there will be none of that. No steamy looks or steamy smirks, and you absolutely will not speak in your Lord Steamy voice."

"I have a different voice for that?" Of course I do, but I love teasing her. "As far as I know, I always sound like me."

"That's true. But you know damn well the tone of your voice changes when you're seducing a woman."

"Am I seducing you? I thought we were having a business-related discussion."

I honestly can't stop myself from smiling in a way she will interpret as seductive. It's just the way I am. All right, maybe I can stop myself—but I don't want to do that. I love watching a woman's demeanor and expression change while she grows more and more aroused. Watching that happen to Avery makes me long to strip her naked and spread that beautiful body across my desk so I can fuck her.

Avery slaps her leather portfolio down on my desk, just like she'd done the other day. "Snap out of it, Hugh."

When did she stand up and walk toward my desk? I'd been so en-meshed in my naughty fantasy that I hadn't noticed. That explains why I flinched when she smacked my desk. "What, darling? Afraid I was away with the fairies for a moment."

"That would have to be porno fairies. I know you were thinking about sex."

"You can read my mind now? I'd better buy some aluminium foil and wrap it around my head."

Her brows squish together. "Why would you do that?"

"To block telepathic frequencies. My mate Reese Dixon married a woman who loves all that paranormal rubbish. I once spent twenty minutes listening to Arden explaining why she believes alien life might exist somewhere in the universe."

Avery still seems disarmingly confused. "What does that have to do with telepathy?"

"Nothing, I suppose."

She stares at me for a bit longer, then her confusion melts into a sly smile. She slants toward me to pat the top of my head. "You go on and duct-tape tinfoil to your head. Won't stop me from figuring you out."

"I thought you were repairing my image, not figuring me out."

"My job requires me to do both."

She returns to her chair, resting her arse on it once again.

Yes, all right, I've been admiring her arse instead of looking at her face. Can't help it. Her figure-hugging skirt makes it impossible for me to ignore her shapely bum—and her shapely legs, not to mention those sexy lips. Everything about her body entrances me.

But I haven't seen her naked yet.

"Wake up," Avery snaps while smacking her palms together to make a sharp noise. "You're doing it again, Lord Sommerleigh. No sex at the office. That means no talking about it, no thinking about it, and no attempts at seduction."

"No thinking about sex? Not sure how you mean to enforce that rule." I roll my chair forward to fold my arms on the desktop. "Considering what we did yesterday, it's too late to scold me for thinking about sex. I've thought about little else since our phone-shag episode."

"Are you deaf? I just told you no sex talk in the office."

"But you just talked about it. When you laid down your no-sex-talk edict."

She throws her head back and growls.

I've never heard a woman emit that sort of noise before. It makes me randy, which seems strange. But I never second guess my lustful impulses. Maybe that's part of the reason I wound up embroiled in a scandal.

Avery shuts her eyes, blows out a breath, and reasserts her business-woman demeanor. "Did you notice anything weird about our date last night?"

"Weird? No. I thought it went rather well."

"It did. But no one looked at you funny."

"Was I meant to give a stand-up comedy performance? No one told me."

She rolls her eyes toward the ceiling and shakes her head. "You are hopeless. I'm trying to help you save your company, but you can't stop cracking jokes and flirting with me."

I sink back in my chair and rub my hands over my face. "Sorry. I know you mean to help, but I have no idea what you were suggesting."

"That nobody looked at you funny. If you were as much of a disgrace as you think, surely someone would've thrown you a disapproving look."

I consider her statement for a moment until I realize the truth. "Yes, you're right. I've been getting dirty looks from the Duke of Wackenbourne's mates, and other people either refuse to look at me or lift their noses and turn away. But no one did anything of the sort in the restaurant—that I noticed. Of course, I was distracted by the bombshell sharing a table with me."

Avery laughs. "Bombshell?"

"That's what you are, darling. Don't deny it. Men must climb over each other to get to you and beg for the honor of a date with the most beautiful woman on earth."

"You're laying it on awfully thick."

"Laying what on? If you mean compliments, I'm afraid I cannot and will not stop doing that. It's all true."

She analyzes me for a moment, her eyes faintly squinted, and I'm sure she means to understand me. But then she crosses her legs, balances her portfolio on her raised thigh, and starts tapping the toe of her shoe in the air again. "Let's get down to business, Lord Sommerleigh."

"I'd love to do that with you."

"No flirting." She wags a finger at me, but her lips form a slight smile. "Behave yourself, or I will…I don't know. Do something. What would make you stop flirting?"

"You could drag me to a funeral, I suppose. Even I would never try it on with anyone during a somber occasion like that."

"So, short of a funeral, I have no way to discourage you."

"Afraid so, pet. It's a reflex, remember?"

"That's part of your problem." She stops tapping her toe and instead drums her fingers on her portfolio. "You need to talk to that Jenkins man. He's your biggest distributor and—"

"Yes, yes, I know. But if the bloke won't talk to me, I have no idea how to get through to him."

"A phone call won't cut it. You need to make him see you."

"Should I text him a picture of me?"

The most beautiful woman on earth growls at me again, louder this time. "You're driving me insane, Hugh. Are you going to cooperate in the salvation of your business? Or would you rather crack jokes and flirt?"

"Are those my only options?"

"Yes."

"Does this edict apply only to work? Or to my personal life too?"

"Work only." She holds up one finger when I start to speak. "That doesn't mean you can behave like you did before the Duke of Wackenbourne decided to ruin you. Act like a responsible, mature adult at all times."

"That sounds like a very dull existence."

"You can make all the jokes you want in private. In public, you need to project a professional image."

"No flirting in public. I should behave like a boring executive. That's what you're telling me."

"Exactly. Have I explained it enough times yet? Some portion of what I said must've sunk into your brain by now."

"Yes, it has." I rub my temples because this conversation is giving me a headache. "Shouldn't I be seen flirting with you in public? You are my fake girlfriend, after all."

"You can flirt, but only in a family-friendly way."

"Whose family is the model for that? They're all different, you know."

"Use your family as the model. They're upstanding aristocrats, right?"

Yes, of course they are. But I'm not. I don't want to explain that to Avery, though she clearly knows the truth. Still, I can't make myself say that one word out loud. It takes me a moment to summon my voice. "Yes. They are respectable, unlike me. I'm a disgrace to my title and the Parrish name."

"No, you are not. That isn't what I was saying."

"What are you trying to tell me, then?"

She just looks at me, holding a neutral expression for so long that I start to wonder if she's developed sudden amnesia. Then she blinks a few times quickly as she rouses from whatever had affected her. Before I have time to process what's happening, she marches around my desk, swivels my chair to face her, and grasps my face in her hands to kiss me. She doesn't push her tongue into my mouth, though. She simply touches her lips to mine and holds that position while my pulse accelerates. We both keep our eyes open too, which feels odd, but in a good way.

Avery breaks the kiss and sits down on my lap, linking her hands at my nape.

"What are you doing?" I ask, though it's bloody obvious. The impetus for this sudden urge to cuddle with me is not as clear. "This isn't workplace behavior."

"No, it's not." She shifts her hands up just enough that her fingertips tease my hair. "You have a severe case of the guilts."

"Is that an incurable illness? I swear I have no idea where I caught it."

"Don't use jokes to avoid the real issue."

"What would you have me do?"

She pecks a kiss on my lips. "You're not ready to hear the answer yet, so I'm giving you a stopgap treatment in the meantime."

Avery relaxes against me, her entire body slack and soft and warm. The light scent of her perfume wafts around me, and when she rests her head on my shoulder, I can't stop myself from releasing all the tension I hadn't realized I was holding in until this moment. I wrap my arms around her.

Then we cuddle. I've never done this before, but I like it.

After a few minutes, Avery slides off my lap and returns to her chair, assuming businesswoman pose again. "Let's get started on a plan to woo Mr. Jenkins back into your good graces."

I sink lower in my chair and wave a hand at her. "Go on. Tell me your plan."

Chapter Ten

Avery

I love cuddling with Hugh Parrish. In fact, I loved it so much that I didn't want to stop, but I knew I had to give up the warmth and comfort of plastering myself to his body. It wasn't a sexual thing, not at all. But I enjoyed that cuddle more than I've enjoyed anything in a long time, which seems crazy. But liking Hugh is not a crime. Maybe my ethics have been stretched lately, thanks to Lord Steamy and my strangely powerful need to help him, not only to save his public image and his company, but to make him feel better.

Yeah, I'm in trouble. And I don't care.

Hugh and I discuss a number of strategies for wooing Mr. Jenkins, but I'm no expert on that side of business. My forte is image consulting—basically PR on steroids. But I think Hugh mostly needs someone on his side who will listen and let him bounce ideas off them. I've become a sounding board, and I don't mind at all. I always do whatever I can to help my clients. With Hugh Parrish, I've gone further. I'm dating him. Regardless of whether we call it fake or not, we went on a real date. Lines are getting blurred, and I should worry about that, but I don't want to worry about anything.

Hugh tells jokes to lighten the mood during our serious conversation about his business, though he doesn't do it to avoid the important stuff. He needs to lighten the mood now and then, and I can't deny he makes me laugh more than anyone else in the world could.

No, I won't fall for him. That would be nuts. I met the man yesterday.

We spend the better part of the day spitballing ideas. Hugh tries calling Jenkins's office again. After that, he needs to attend a board meeting, so I go back to my hotel to brainstorm even more ideas for Hugh. Maybe I shouldn't be this invested in my client's life. But I care what happens to him, not just his company, and I'm done trying to hide that fact. I care about every client, but Lord Sommerleigh is... I don't know. Special, I suppose. But I refuse to waste brainpower on figuring out why. Once I've gotten Hugh over the worst of his problems, then maybe I'll think about why I agreed to fake date him.

For the sake of my sanity and my professional ethics, I insist we meet only at his office, not my hotel suite or his apartment. Our dates are the exception, but I do ask him to drop me off at the door to my hotel rather than the door to my suite.

"But we're meant to be dating," he says when I share my decision with him the next day. "A proper viscount walks his date to her door."

"Please, Lord Sommerleigh, let's keep it professional." Yes, I've reasserted my dictate that I will refer to him only as Lord Sommerleigh, except on our dates.

"Are you afraid you'll lose control and beg me to shag you?" He crosses his heart with two fingers. "I swear on my father's grave that I shall not attempt to seduce you when I walk you to your door."

"No, Lord Sommerleigh. Drop me off at the hotel entrance."

"I love it when you order me to do things. Though in this case, I'm not entirely pleased with your pronouncement." He sighs with melodramatic disappointment. "But I shall heed your command."

Over the next week, we spend most of our time ensconced in his office hashing out ideas. Hugh tries repeatedly to get through to Phillip Jenkins, but the man refuses to see or speak to him. Jenkins's executive assistant loves Hugh and the decadent candies he sent her, but even that connection isn't enough to get him an audience with Jenkins himself.

What has he been told about Hugh? Jenkins might be good friends with the Duke of Wackenbourne, or maybe the reason has nothing to do with Hugh. I don't know, and we will never find out the answer if we can't get in to see the man.

Yeah, I'm now thinking about me and Hugh as one unit, as…a couple. The realization sends a tingle rushing over my skin, but I can't decide if I'm excited or terrified by the prospect. We're a pretend couple. But sometimes it doesn't feel fake.

We go on two more dates during the week and over the weekend. But on Monday morning, we get news we've been hoping to hear.

Phillip Jenkins has agreed to meet with us.

"Will you come with me to Jenkins's office?" Hugh asks. "I know it's not in your job description. But now that you've helped me figure out a plan, I feel, ah…"

"Anxious? It's okay, you can say that out loud. I won't make fun of you. Feeling nervous is understandable, considering what's at stake." Though he's hiding it well, I notice little signs that tell me he's more anxious than he wants me to know. So I walk around his desk to sit on his lap with my arms around his neck. "Yes, I'll go with you for moral support."

"Thank you. Not sure I could do this alone."

"Of course you could. But I'm happy to hold your hand during the meeting, literally or figuratively. Whatever you need."

He lifts his brows. "Whatever I need? That's a dangerous thing to say to the man who's accused of seducing every married woman in the country."

"You aren't like that." I kiss his cheek. "And everyone will have forgotten about that nonsense by the time I'm done polishing up your image. You already got a positive mention in a newspaper."

"Yes, it said 'Lord Sommerleigh appears to be behaving like a gentleman these days.' It was in the style section, and the journalist spent four paragraphs describing my clothing."

"It's a start. Be grateful for that."

"Of course I'm grateful. Praise for my suit is much better than snide comments about my sex life."

"Even a small win is still a victory."

Our meeting with Jenkins won't happen for three days. That leaves Hugh with plenty of time to get anxious. In the days leading up to the meeting, he gets progressively and visibly more nervous. He even stops cracking jokes. He doesn't try to seduce me, either. He behaves like a true gentleman, which I would love if I didn't know he acts that way mostly because he's worried about the meeting.

I wouldn't want him to be a complete gentleman. Having a naughty side is one of his best qualities.

The day arrives, and we put on our best business outfits. I literally hold Hugh's hand while we walk into the building. But then he lets go, giving me a tight smile, and I know the anxiety has hit him again.

"You'll do fine," I whisper to him as we approach the desk occupied by Jenkins's executive assistant.

The young woman smiles at us. "Good morning, Lord Sommerleigh. And you must be Avery Hahn. I'm Megan."

Since we hadn't wanted to ambush Jenkins with my presence, Hugh had informed the man that his "business consultant" would accompany him.

Megan ushers us to the closed door to Jenkins's office and swings it open for us, waving for us to enter first. She leaves the door open as she grabs a notepad and pen from her desk, then follows us into the office, where she takes a seat near her boss.

Hugh and I don't sit down yet. First, we need to introduce ourselves.

But our host gets there first. The gray-haired man behind the desk gives us a polite smile as he stands to offer Hugh his hand. "Good afternoon, Lord Sommerleigh. It's a pleasure to see you again."

"Thank you," Hugh says while shaking the man's hand. "I appreciate you giving us a bit of your time."

Jenkins waves to the chairs. "Please, sit down."

And so the meeting begins.

Hugh gives our host a seemingly relaxed smile that matches his posture, but I notice the faintest wrinkles around his eyes that show how worried he really is. As much as I want to hug him, I can't do that during a business meeting. I'll wait until later to throw my arms around him.

"I know why you're here," Jenkins tells Hugh. "I imagine you saw the article."

"Yes. It suggested you might be on the verge of canceling our contract. Is that true?"

Jenkins clasps his hands on his desk and gazes down at them. "I'm afraid so."

My stomach drops like a stone, and I can only imagine how much Hugh must be freaking out on the inside. Outwardly, he still seems relaxed and professional. But those lines around his eyes have deepened.

"May I ask what changed your mind about Sommerleigh Sweets?" Hugh asks. "Our companies have enjoyed a prosperous and friendly partnership for many years."

We both know what made Jenkins change his mind, but Hugh has to ask.

Jenkins stares down at his hands for a moment in silence. Then he raises his head. "I want you to know that I don't judge my employees or my business associates based on how they conduct their personal lives. As long as they do their jobs well, the rest is none of my concern."

Oh yeah, I hear a "but" coming.

"Though you and I haven't had a great deal of personal contact," Jenkins continues, "I've always liked and respected you as a business owner and as a person."

Here it comes…

"But I can't be seen to condone your recent behavior." Jenkins sits back in his chair and exhales a heavy sigh. "I'm sorry, Lord Sommerleigh. Yes, I am on the verge of deciding to cancel our contract with Sommerleigh Sweets."

Hugh clears his throat. "I understand. But perhaps you would give me a chance to explain."

"Not sure that would help. I've received complaints from certain peers who are pressuring me to sever my company's relationship with yours."

I can guess who those "peers" are—the Duke of Wackenbourne and his nasty friends.

"Whatever you've heard," Hugh says, "it's not entirely accurate. I don't claim to be a saint, but I would never do the things a certain someone has accused me of doing."

"Yes, I understand that. And your family has always been a strong business partner for us. But…" Jenkins scratches his cheek and glances out the window before looking at Hugh again. "In consideration of our long-term business relationship, I will take some time to mull over the issues. That's the best I can offer right now."

"And I appreciate that you're granting us that much. I could offer you a number of hefty inducements, but I'd much rather you reach a conclusion on your own."

"Thank you, Lord Sommerleigh. I will have an answer for you next week."

Hugh and I say goodbye to Jenkins and walk out of the office. We had both known going into this meeting that Jenkins wouldn't vow to stand by Sommerleigh Sweets no matter what. He runs a business, and his personal opinion of Hugh doesn't matter. If the Duke of Wackenbourne and his cronies put pressure on Jenkins, the man will have to give in for the sake of his company and his employees.

We board the elevator and find ourselves alone in the car.

I throw my arms around Hugh. "I'm so sorry that didn't go the way we'd both hoped."

"Don't apologize. We knew he wouldn't make a decision today, and it's unlikely he will decide in our favor."

Maybe it's weird that we both refer to his meeting and his company as if we're both invested in his business, as if we're partners. And maybe I shouldn't care this much about Hugh's well-being when I've known him for a week. But I do care, and feelings rarely adhere to logic or a predefined time line.

I keep my arms around Hugh until we reach the ground floor. Then we walk out of the elevator like two business professionals. We don't climb into a limo. Hugh told me the other day that he'd hired a limousine because he thought I would want that. When I assured him that I don't care what kind of car he has, he seemed surprised, but only for a moment. I also told him he should act like himself rather than trying to impress all those people who are more than happy to think the worst of him. Behaving like a gentleman, like his true self, will do more good than fancy limos and schmoozing with stuck-up rich people.

That means when we exit Jenkins Foods, we head for a car parked in the lot outside. No driver waits for us. Hugh helps me into the passenger side, then climbs into the driver's seat.

My next task might be the hardest of all. It's time to make him tell me about Scotland.

Chapter Eleven

Hugh

I settle into the driver's seat and shove the key into the ignition, but I freeze while still holding onto the key. Avery keeps telling me wealth doesn't matter and I need to impress everyone with my personality and my gentlemanly behavior. But I can't help feeling a bit odd about my car after those conversations. That's why I find myself looking at her and wincing. "Sorry. I don't own a normal car. Just the one my parents gave me when I turned eighteen. That would be this vehicle."

"A Jaguar sedan is hardly abnormal for an aristocrat who has money."

"But I thought you wanted me to seem normal."

"When did I say that? I told you to act like yourself and behave like a gentleman."

I twist the key in the ignition, and the engine rumbles to life. "But that sounded like—"

"Don't interpret what I say. Just listen and take it at face value."

"Sorry. I know I do that too often. Redefining your words, I mean." I back the car out of the space, which gives me an excuse to avoid looking at her. "I'll try to do better. But you did tell me to stop flirting."

"With anyone except for me, your fake girlfriend. That doesn't mean you can't be yourself."

"Right. I'm interpreting your words again, aren't I? Blimey, reinventing yourself is bloody hard work."

"Yes, it is."

Well, after the way I've cocked up my life, I deserve to suffer. The fact that I've learned my lesson makes no difference. I need to convince everyone else, all those people I don't even like, that I'm not a craven seducer.

Just as I put my foot on the accelerator, about to start driving, Avery lays a hand on my arm. "Let's go to your apartment."

I glance at her, and I'm positive I appear stunned. "My flat? Why? You said we should never do that."

"No, I did not say never. Now that we've established ourselves as a couple in public, we need to talk about a few things." She gives my arm a light squeeze. "Think of this as two friends having a conversation, not as torture, and you'll do fine."

Saying I will "do fine" doesn't ease my anxiety at all because I know what she means to interrogate me about—Scotland.

Just as I turn my head toward the front of the car, Avery grasps my face and forces me to look at her. "You need to do this, Hugh. Not for me, but for you. It's time to unburden yourself."

"I'll try, but—"

She presses her mouth to mine, firmly, for long enough that my cock is waking up and asking if it's time to shag her yet. Fortunately, she pulls away before I develop an embarrassing and unmistakable problem. I've never gotten embarrassed because I have an erection at an inconvenient time or place, but since I met Avery, I've become afflicted with a ridiculous amount of anxiety about everything.

Yes, she'll want to sleep with me now, won't she? A pathetic lump of a man is terribly attractive to women.

"Take me to your flat, Hugh," she says. When I just sit here like an ice sculpture, she points down at my feet. "That means you need to press down on the gas pedal."

"Oh. Yes. Sorry." I start the car rolling, which at least gives me a reason not to glance at her. "Thank you again for going with me to that meeting. I failed miserably at charming Mr. Jenkins, but at least I'll have an answer sometime next week."

"You didn't fail miserably. We both agreed yesterday that trying to charm Jenkins wouldn't work. You needed to be yourself, and you excelled at that."

"Excelled? I barely said two complete sentences."

"You said more than that. Being too hard on yourself is a bad habit."

"It's my fault Sommerleigh Sweets is in trouble, so I'm not being too hard on myself."

Avery sighs with what sounds like disappointment, then she turns her attention to the view outside her window. We both remain silent for the rest of our drive back to my building, and we've still said nothing when I unlock the door to my flat. I gesture for her to enter first, and she gives me a kind smile. Perfect. The woman I desperately need to shag is gazing at me with kindness, not desire, which probably means she feels sorry for me.

I've barely flirted with her over the past week. Am I losing my touch? Maybe I'm just losing my mind. Not sure which option is worse.

The second I shut the door, Avery flings her arms around me.

I gingerly rest my palms on her back. "Ah, what are you doing?"

"Hugging you." She raises her head to aim those beautiful, deep-blue eyes at me. "You needed it."

Wonderful. Now I'm so pathetic that she feels compelled to comfort me. "You don't need to do that. I won't collapse on the floor and start sobbing about what a useless whingeing arse I've become."

"You aren't useless, and you don't complain." Avery steps back and clasps my hand. "Let's go sit on the sofa together so you can spill your guts to me in comfort."

"Oh yes, you make it sound so like so bloody much fun."

"Sarcasm is a good sign. It means you haven't completely given up." She splays her palms on my chest and fingers my tie. "Maybe you need an incentive."

"Yes, I do. Grab a bottle of Scotch from the kitchen, and I'll drink the whole ruddy thing. Then I'll tell you anything you want to know."

"Uh-uh-uh. No cheating." She begins to undo my tie, her gaze riveted to the task. "Getting drunk won't make you feel any better."

"Have I told you how much I love the skirt suits you wear? They're sexy as hell."

"Your flirting won't distract me from my goal." She has my tie undone now, and she unhooks the top button on my shirt. Then she grasps one end of my tie in each hand. When she lifts her head, a sensual smile curves her lips. "Wanna have sex?"

"What? I—Well, of course I want to. But I doubt I can manage it right now."

"Hmm." She starts walking backward while still holding my tie in both hands, which pulls me forward with her as if she's leashed me. "Let's find out what you can manage."

I let her lead me to the sofa, but I can't watch where we're going, not with her hips swaying and that hungry look on her face. When she catches her bottom lip between her teeth and releases it slowly, my cock jerks. Avery tosses my tie away and shoves me backward with one hand on my chest.

And I drop onto the sofa.

She shimmies her hips, hiking her skirt up to her waist, and sits on my lap.

I finger the edge of her lace knickers. "Your plan might work. Don't stop now."

She slides backward just enough to rest her arse on my knees. Then she unzips my trousers and slips her hand inside to wrap her fingers around my cock. Just as I start to get firm, the worst thing happens. I start thinking about my problems, the shame I've brought on my family, the way I've avoided my best mate, and the terrible things that might happen if I can't save my company.

And my blossoming erection wilts.

I let my head fall back against the sofa, shut my eyes, and groan like the miserable sod I am. "Bugger me. I can't even get a leg over anymore."

The woman sitting on my lap pecks a kiss on my lips. "It's okay. I'm not upset. Actually, I kind of expected this reaction, but it was worth a shot."

"Nothing like this has ever happened to me before." I raise my head, but I can't meet her gaze. "Well, maybe once or twice when I was a randy teenager. But never in my adult life."

She slides off my lap, tugs her skirt down, and settles onto the cushion beside me. "It's time."

I could pretend I have no idea what she means, but that would only delay the inevitable. "You want to know about Scotland. First, you should know this will be a short story, not an epic novel. Callum and I have been best mates for years. Nothing and no one could get between us—until Kate Wagner came into our lives and everything went sideways. What happened was mostly my fault."

"Tell me about it."

"How it's my fault?" I grunt. "I'm a blind moron who couldn't see what would've been bloody obvious to anyone else. I swear I'm not as dimwitted as it will sound like I am once I've told you everything. Callum's brother sent him to Inverness to convalesce after a knee injury, but his physical therapist turned out to be a beautiful American woman. I met her when I flew to Scotland to provide moral support for my best mate."

"And the American woman was Kate."

"Yes. Callum swore he had no interest in her, so I tried to win her over. Kate kept insisting she wasn't attracted to me, but being a bloody-minded fool, I refused to believe I had no chance with her." I stare down at my lap because I can't watch the expression on Avery's face while I confess the rest. "I was staying with Callum at his cousin's apartment, so I had ample opportunity to realize what was going on around me. But I convinced myself it was rubbish. Callum could not be sleeping with Kate after he'd sworn he didn't even like her. My best mate wouldn't lie to me."

"But he did."

I nod and pick at the seam of the sofa cushion. "I found out they'd been sleeping together on the day Kate decided to fly back to America. Callum slugged me in the gut because I wouldn't get out of the way. He meant to rush to the airport and stop her. She was already gone, but it turned out the MacTaggart clan had whisked her away to their castle in the back of beyond."

Avery snuggles up to me, her legs tucked under her, and lays a hand on my shoulder.

Though I can see her peripherally, I still can't make myself look at her. "The MacTaggarts and some of my British mates, along with a few Americans, sort of kidnapped me. They and their wives arranged a series of bizarre tests designed to force me and Callum to work through our issues. They called it 'radical intervention.' The tactic succeeded. We're best mates again."

"I hear a 'but' in that statement. Go on, tell me the rest and get it off your chest."

Sighing, I shut my eyes for a moment before I aim my gaze straight at hers. "But I haven't seen Callum since, and I've avoided talking to him on the phone. He called me last week. We did chat to each other, but not for long. I still can't reconcile what I learned about myself in Scotland with who I thought I was."

"What do you mean?"

I shouldn't do it, but I feel a strong need to take comfort from her. So I slip an arm around her waist and pull her closer. "Kate and I had a serious conversation in that castle. She helped me realize that I didn't really want her. I couldn't accept that, for the first time, I had failed to seduce a woman. She's not just *any* woman, though. Kate Wagner is quite remarkable. I thought—It's bloody stupid."

"Don't do that, Hugh. Stop hiding from embarrassing truths."

What else can I do? I grimace so hard that I'm squeezing my eyes shut. "I thought she might be the sort of woman I could spend the rest of my life with. Never wanted that before, but with her…I let myself consider the possibility."

"Do you still feel that way about Kate?"

"No. But I think I haven't completely recovered from the shock of realizing I do want to find the right woman and settle down. That will never happen now. No one would want to marry a disgraced viscount who destroyed his company and his family."

Avery kisses my cheek. "Thank you for sharing all of that with me."

"To say 'you're welcome' seems bizarre."

Delicate laughter bubbles out of her. "Yeah, I guess it does. Try not to worry so much about what might happen and focus on doing what you can to fix things today, tomorrow, one day at a time."

"I'll try. Strangely, I do feel better after spilling my guts to you."

"Glad to hear it." She fingers the unhooked button of my shirt. "I have a confession too."

"You don't need to tell me anything personal just because I shared my humiliating story."

"But I want to share things with you." She frees the second button on my shirt. "The truth is, I'm not as satisfied with my job as I let everyone think. I used to love it, back when I had a diverse clientele instead of working exclusively for incredibly rich people. Somehow, that just kind of happened."

"Because you're brilliant at your job. Everyone wants your help."

"And I'm happy to help them. But I feel like I've lost something in the process. My life has become a series of airline tickets and meetings with multimillionaires."

I crush my mouth to hers, but I don't try to slip my tongue between her lips. I only want to feel her skin against mine, the softness of her mouth, and the warmth of her that radiates into me. "I think we have similar problems. Maybe we can help each other."

"How?"

"Not sure yet. Let's both think about it." I rise and offer her my hand. "For now, let's go into the kitchen. You can watch me make dinner for you."

"It's kind of early for dinner."

"Rubbish." I sweep her up in my arms. "It's never too early to enjoy a decadent feast."

"Not hungry enough for that."

I wink. "Did I say I meant to feast on food? No, love, it's you I hunger for."

Chapter Twelve

Avery

He hungers for me. When Hugh spoke those words, I felt deliciously warm and ready for anything he wanted to do to me. But after he carried me to the bar and set me down on a stool, we both realized we're too raw for sex. Confessions take a lot out of a person. Hugh told me about his time in Scotland at last, and I finally get why he's been so off balance lately. I hadn't known him before his life changed, but his mom told me enough that I know he used to be confident and in command.

Now he worries about everything.

We enjoy an early dinner, but then I go back to my hotel. Hugh insists on driving me there. He walks me to my suite and kisses me good night, though he keeps it chaste. Hugh kisses my hand too, then walks away.

I dream about him, though not the way I would've expected. In my subconscious fantasies, we hold hands and take romantic walks together. We cuddle on the sofa, make each other laugh, and do all the things a not-phony couple would do. I wake up in the morning feeling weird, like I actually did all those things with Hugh, but I didn't.

Would he want a real relationship with me? Do I want that with him? Our lives are so complicated. Not sure we could ever merge our lifestyles. I travel wherever clients need me while Hugh clearly prefers to stay home—in London or at Sommerleigh. I told Hugh I've gotten tired of my vagabond lifestyle, but I neglected to mention that I'm terrified of trying to change that. What if I lose my upscale clients and can't attract normal ones? Worst of all, what if my fake relationship with Hugh ruins my business?

I'd wanted to sleep with Hugh yesterday. But that's a bad idea. I can't help wanting him, and I seem incapable of resisting the man, whether he tries to seduce me or I try to get him hot and bothered. From now on, I need to behave like he's my client—when we're alone. Our fake dating can continue, but it will not bleed into our client and consultant relationship.

Never mind that phone sex incident. Or the fact I removed his tie and unbuttoned his shirt yesterday. Or the times I kissed him. And it absolutely does not matter that I like him and feel...protective of him. No, that means nothing.

He's my client, period.

Now that I've reasserted my ethics, I get dressed and eat breakfast, then head out the door intending to go to Hugh's office. I halt on the threshold of my suite, with my hand on the knob, ready to shut the door. Where am I going? It's Saturday. Hugh won't be in his office today. Last weekend, we went on a date on Saturday night and didn't see each other on Sunday. I'd assumed he needed a break from seeing me, and I'd been fine with that. I had not missed him. But last night I dreamed about Hugh, and this morning I rushed out of my suite intending to see him, though I have no legitimate reason to do that.

I am not falling for Hugh Parrish. It's impossible.

Since I have nowhere I need to go, I walk back into my suite and change into sweats and a T-shirt, then I watch TV. Wow, is that boring. When I get sick of reality shows about people hunting for luxury vacation homes, I pick up my cell phone and start to punch in a number—Hugh's number. *No, no, no, you need distance from him, not cuddle time with Lord Steamy.* I swear I used to have self-control, but I seem to have misplaced it on the flight from New York to London.

I call my brother instead.

"Avery?" Derek says sleepily when he answers his phone. "It's four o'clock in the morning."

"Oh no, I forgot. I'm so sorry I woke you. Go back to sleep."

"You forgot what time zone you're in?" Rustling suggests he's sitting up or at least coming to full wakefulness. He doesn't sound sleepy anymore when he says, "Avery Hahn always knows where she is, what she's doing, and what time it is. You don't do scattered-brained."

"I am feeling a little off today. It's nothing to worry about."

"What has that client of yours done to you? Must be running you ragged."

"Honestly, you're being ridiculous. I'm tired, that's all."

Since I muted the TV but didn't turn it off, I can see the spoiled people on the screen turning their noses up at perfectly nice houses. I wouldn't mind buying a house on a tropical beach somewhere if I could spend my days lounging on the sand while Hugh massages suntan lotion into my skin.

Ugh. How did Hugh get into my daydream?

"Avery," Derek snaps with enough volume that I jerk my phone away from my ear for a split second. "Are you listening?"

"No, sorry, I wasn't."

"Okay, now I know something is wrong. Must be that mysterious client of yours."

I make a frustrated noise and thump my hand on the sofa cushion. "Butt out of my life, would you? I'm a grown woman, and I don't need my big brother to fix my life."

"Your life needs fixing?" Derek pauses, then his voice drops to a near whisper. "It's that Lord Steamy guy, isn't it? I trolled the London tabloids a few days ago, and I saw you with him. Hoped you would tell me you're involved with that guy on your own, but you haven't. I just gave you at least three openings in our conversation, but you still didn't tell me about him. What kind of douche calls himself Lord Steamy, anyway?"

Well, now that he knows... "His name is Hugh Parrish, the Viscount Sommerleigh. He's not a douche, and I can take care of myself."

"You're doing him, aren't you?"

"Stop it, Derek." I haven't technically had sex with Hugh, except for the phone variety, so I'm not lying to my brother. I think. "Go back to sleep. We can talk about this more later."

"Are you in bed with him right now?"

"For heaven's sake. That is none of your business."

He grunts. "That means yes."

"No, it means I'm alone on the sofa in my hotel suite watching stupid real estate shows. Hugh is on the other side of town in his apartment. Has been all night."

"Glad to hear it. But I still think I should check on you."

"You just did. I'm fine. Go back to sleep, Derek. Goodbye."

I hang up before he can say anything else. Calling my brother had been a bad idea. But he won't do anything rash like fly to London to rescue me from Lord Steamy. No, Derek will cool down and realize he overreacted.

For the rest of the day, I distract myself by going for a long walk to admire historic buildings and modern architecture, then I eat lunch at a cute little bistro. After that, I go sightseeing. Visiting Buckingham Palace to watch the changing of the guard isn't much fun by myself, so I give up on exploring the city. Hugh lives here, so he could serve as my tour guide and would know all the best places to visit, but I can't risk seeing him again. Not yet. Not so soon after our intimate confessions yesterday and the way I tried to seduce him. I need to wait until Monday. By then, I'll have gotten over this weird fixation with Hugh Parrish.

And yes, from now on I will refer to him only by his title.

With my boundaries reset, I go back to my suite and contemplate the room service menu—until my cell phone rings. I answer it without thinking. "Avery Hahn."

"It's me, darling."

"Hugh—Lord Sommerleigh? Why are you calling me?"

"We're back to Lord Sommerleigh? I thought after yesterday we were closer than just business associates. We have a more intimate relationship now."

"We've let our business dealings bleed into our personal lives, but that's over now. I'll be your fake girlfriend until you can find a real one. That shouldn't take too long since you're, um, good at, well, that sort of thing."

"It's called seduction, love."

"Yes, I know that. From now on, we will see each other only at your office or on our dates. There will be none of that...other stuff."

He chuckles. "Other stuff? You mean sex. The problem I had last night won't be repeated. After a good night's sleep, I feel refreshed and ready for anything."

"Good for you. Why don't you try going to a party or something on your own? Let the other aristocrats see who you really are."

"Without my best girl on my arm? No one would believe that. If you aren't there, they will assume you've thrown me over."

He's right. I know that, but I can't see him until Monday. I need another day to widen the distance between us. That will work, right? I'm not being desperate and half-crazy.

I take a deep breath and exhale it slowly, releasing the panic. "I will see you on Monday, Lord Sommerleigh."

"But I miss you, darling. I want to slide my hands under your skirt and—"

"Not wearing a skirt."

He sighs with a touch of melodrama. "If you insist on languishing in your suite alone, I won't bother you anymore. But if you change your mind, I'll be in my flat all evening."

"Good night, Hugh."

Only after I've hung up do I realize I used his first name again. *Gah.* He drives me insane.

Why had I confessed to Hugh that my life has left me feeling unfulfilled? At least I didn't blurt out that I'm lonely. For a long time, I've tried to deny it, though in the recesses of my mind I recognize the truth. Is that why I can't keep my hands or lips off Hugh Parrish? I need to know the answers to those questions. But there's only one way to make that happen.

I need to see Hugh.

And if talking to him in person leads to incredible sex, well, that's the risk I'll take. I almost laugh, but that would be weird. It's my own joke in my own head.

I change clothes and grab a taxi.

By the time I reach Hugh's building, I expect I'll panic and run away any second. But that doesn't happen. I calmly ride in the elevator to his floor and calmly approach the door. When I grant myself a moment to realize what I'm about to do, I feel not even a twinge of guilt or anxiety. Huh. That's not what I expected.

Panic-free, I roll my shoulders back and knock on the door.

It swings open seconds later, and Hugh stares at me like he can't believe I'm here. His lids flutter, but that must be a sign of surprise instead of grit in his eyes. "Avery? I wasn't expecting to see you, but I'm glad you're here."

"Me too."

I follow him into the living room and choose the armchair instead of the sofa this time. I can't throw myself at him if I'm sitting three feet away with a table between us. Well, I probably can't do that. I might need to downgrade "probably" to "maybe." Oh, who am I kidding? My chances are slim to none that I can restrain my lust for the Viscount Sommerleigh.

But I sit in the armchair anyway.

Hugh drops onto the sofa in the exact middle of it. Then he leans back, hooks one ankle over the other knee, and spreads both arms across the sofa's back. He's wearing the shirt and slacks from one of his suits but no shoes.

"Are you going somewhere?" I ask. "Need shoes if you are."

"Don't need to go anywhere." His lips curve into a smile so hot that it makes my nipples tighten. "You came for me."

Of course he means those words as a double entendre. His tone makes it impossible to deny that fact. "If you mean I came here to see you, then you're right."

"I meant that and the much more enjoyable interpretation."

"We shouldn't have sex, Hugh. I wanted to talk to you and figure out why..." My voice trails off because I suddenly realize I can't tell him the reason I'm here. Right now, Lord Steamy is operating at a low simmer. If he cranks it up to a full head of steam, I'm in trouble. "Never mind. I shouldn't have come here."

"You haven't done that yet, darling."

"Must you turn everything into seduction?" I stand up. "Sorry I bothered you."

"Don't leave." He pats the sofa cushion beside him. "Let's discuss whatever it is like adults. I will do my best not to flirt with you."

"Okay." If I sound hesitant, I have good reason. Sitting right next to Hugh... That's dangerous. But I do it anyway. I march around the coffee table and rest my bottom on the cushion beside him, leaving as much space between us as possible—which means about six inches. "I, um, well..."

"Just tell me, Avery. I can handle it."

"I told you yesterday that my life hasn't been quite what I'd hoped for. Used to love what I do, but lately I feel less than satisfied."

"Yes, I remember."

"And I've also realized I can't keep my hands off you." I have no control over the tingle that sweeps through me when I inadvertently lean back and feel his arm behind my head, his fingers brushing my shoulder. "But I finally figured out why."

"Tell me, love."

"You're irresistible."

Chapter Thirteen

Hugh

A m I?" Her statement, spoken in a businesswoman-like tone, seems odd—especially coming from Avery Hahn. I doubt she actually finds me irresistible. It's more likely that she gave in to her own passionate nature at last and I happened to be the man who had the privilege of benefiting from her realization. "I've been told similar things before, but only by women who batted their lashes at me. They weren't serious. When a woman says that to me, I know she just wants to get me naked so she can brag to her mates about how she shagged a viscount."

"I don't care about your title, Hugh."

"Yes, I know that. But you called me irresistible."

She hunches her shoulders and averts her gaze to the windows. "I can't resist you. That's what I meant."

"And it bothers you. Lusting for me, that is."

"It used to." She aims those luminous eyes directly at me. "But not anymore. I've come to terms with the fact I need you to fuck me over and over until I can't move or speak anymore."

A sensation I have never experienced before seizes me. I think I'm…stunned. Avery has a way of surprising me with deceptively simple statements, but this time, she has well and truly shocked me. Other women have begged me to shag them, but always in a cheeky way. Avery seems quite serious about wanting me to fuck her all night.

I want that too, but… "When I rang you an hour ago, you swore we would only see each other at the office or on our supposedly fake dates."

"Changed my mind."

"So quickly? I don't want you to regret it in the morning."

"This decision didn't happen an hour ago. I've known for a while that I need to be with you at least once, though I didn't consciously recognize that until today."

Yes, that sounds too much like the night when the Duchess of Wackenbourne whispered into my ear that she wanted me to shag her until dawn. Whether she regretted it later, I can't say. But I did, and I do not want Avery to feel that way in the morning.

She lays a hand on my cheek, trailing her fingertips down to my lips. "I won't regret this. I panicked briefly when I had my epiphany, but now I'm ready. In case you haven't noticed, I am insanely attracted to you, have been from the start. We live in different worlds, Hugh, so this can't ever become more than a night of hot sex."

"Only one night?"

"Does it matter? I thought you liked to be spontaneous and let things just happen."

"I do." Why am I arguing about this? She wants me, I want her, and we are both unattached adults. So I pull her close and whisper, "Let's do it." Her mouth slides into the sexiest, most erotic smile I've ever seen. That expression gives me an odd feeling in my chest, but I can't think about that right now. My cock won't let me. "Get up. We need to undress."

"Here in the living room?"

"Yes, darling, here." I stand, offering her my hands and helping her up. "In the living room, with the curtains open. The trees conceal most of the windows, but I can't promise no one will see us."

"Don't care." She pulls out the clip she'd used to hold her hair back and lets those luscious blonde waves fall over her shoulders. "I need you inside me right now."

I can't help chuckling. "We need to remove our clothes first, pet."

She hesitates in the middle of unhooking the top button of her blouse and stares at me for a moment. Then she flips the blouse up and over her head, flinging it away. The garment lands on the armchair. I stand frozen, gawping at her while she pushes her skirt down over her hips and kicks it away. Avery now stands a few feet from me, wearing only a lacy powder-blue bra and matching knickers.

Oh, and sexy stilettos.

But she kicks those off too.

When I reach for her, she scuttles backward and waves a finger at me. "No, no, no. You get naked first."

"You haven't finished. You're still wearing a bra and knickers."

"Get naked, Hugh. Now."

She is definitely not panicking anymore.

"Have I told you how much I love it when a woman tells me what she wants?" I ask while I unbutton my shirt. "Especially when that woman is you."

"Talk dirty to me. Please."

"If you insist." I shrug out of my shirt and toss it away. The shirt lands on top of Avery's blouse. "See those windows? I mean to push you against that glass, facing away, and push inside you so slowly that you'll be panting for me. Your tits will be crushed to the window, your entire body too, while I fuck you."

"Oh, yes."

The tips of her nipples jut through the flimsy fabric of her bra. I unhook my belt and pull it free of the loops one by one. "Your cream will be all over the window, darling. Then I'll flip you around and take you again, hard and fast, but I won't let you come yet. No, I mean to stretch you across the coffee table and fuck you there so you can feel the smooth, cool surface against your skin."

She skims her palms up her belly and cups her breasts, pinching her nipples.

"Fuck, Avery," I all but growl. "Don't get started without me."

"Can't help it. Watching you undress while you're talking dirty makes me so hot that I almost can't stand it." As if to prove her point, she skates her hands back down her belly and slips one between her thighs to palm her mound through her knickers. "I need you now, Hugh, so hurry it up."

I get rid of my shoes, hurling them across the room, and shed the rest of my clothing so fast that I'm breathing hard by the time I finish.

Avery gives me a sexily teasing smile. "Gee, I assumed you wouldn't have anything on under your slacks."

"Sometimes I don't. Today, I wore pants."

"I know. But I was talking about your underwear."

"Those are my pants, darling. That's what we call them over here in the real world."

"Are all you Brits so arrogantly certain that your country is the best in the world?"

"Yes." I saunter up to her and reach behind her back to unhook her bra. "Have you shagged a Brit before?"

"Never."

"A virgin? Well, I will make sure you get the full English."

"I thought that meant breakfast."

"Yes, it does." And I have no idea why I said that. Avery has me so wound up that I can't remember what words mean anymore. But I know how to recover from my blunder. I toss her bra away and push my hand inside her knickers. "I plan to devour you, darling, one lick at a time."

"But it's evening," she says while struggling to catch her breath. "Your breakfast metaphor doesn't work."

"Haven't you ever ordered breakfast for dinner?" Enough of this ruddy metaphor. I tear her knickers off. Luckily, the lace fabric is flimsy enough that I can rip it. Her knickers land on the sofa as I grasp her hand. "Come with me to the windows. I mean to make good on everything I told you I want to do to your body."

She yanks her hand free of mine and trots over to the floor-to-ceiling windows, plastering her body to the glass. "I'm ready."

I laugh as I walk over there to join her. "Yes, you are. And I love your enthusiasm."

Her brows wrinkle. "Aren't you forgetting something?"

"What?"

She glances down at my cock. "Condom."

"Oh. Yes." I race to the end table and jerk the drawer open to retrieve a packet. Once I've rolled the condom on, I return to the windows and Avery. "I'm ready now too."

"Please, hurry up."

"Well, I never deny a woman what she needs." I kick her feet further apart, grasp her hips, and plunge into her slick heat. "Fuck, Avery, you're so wet it's dribbling down my cock."

"Weeks of unrequited lust will do that."

I rest my chin on her shoulder and start thrusting, slowly at first, then harder and faster while she alternately moans and cries out every time I lunge into her. With all of her glued to the windows, her skin makes little squeaking sounds. She curls her fingers on the glass and squeezes her eyes shut while I grunt and groan, pumping with such vigor that my heart pounds and sweat runs down my temples.

"Oh God," she moans. "I'm about to—"

She lets out a sharp cry just as her inner muscles clench my cock. I hiss in a breath and keep thrusting, even while the pressure inside me mounts every second, and I know I won't last much longer. The sensation of her muscles milking me over and over does me in. An electric shock ripples down my spine and straight into my cock, setting off swift spasms that push me over the edge. I come while buried deep inside her beautiful body, thrusting a few more times until I'm finished.

Though I'd promised to flip her around and take her again, I decide to skip that bit. I'll do it next time. I can't move, anyway. With my chin still on her shoulder, I fight to regain my breath. After a moment, I manage to speak, though my voice comes out slightly hoarse. "Well, darling, are you satisfied now?"

"Yes, oh God, yes. Thank you."

"My pleasure, love. Should we try the coffee table next? Or do you need a lie-down?"

"Don't you dare stop." She wriggles around to face me. "I'm expecting the full English Lord Steamy treatment."

"I never want to disappoint a woman. And I haven't fulfilled my promises yet." I pick her up and take three steps backward. "But I have made good on some of them. Take a look."

She glances at the window, and when she notices the smears on the glass, she grins at me.

That expression gives me another strange feeling in my chest.

I carry her over to the coffee table and lay her down on her back with her calves dangling over the edge. As I kneel in front of her, she licks her lips like she wants to devour me the way I plan to devour her. Well, she can do that later. I still have unfulfilled plans for her body, so I tickle the soles of her feet. "Bend your knees. Heels on the table."

She obeys my command without asking why. "You do things backwards, hey? Most men want to get oral over with right away."

"Over with? You've been with the wrong kinds of men. Do I seem like that sort of arse?"

"No. You are nothing like any other guy I've known."

I drag the tips of my index fingers down the insides of her thighs, barely touching her skin, and she shivers faintly. "When I make love to a woman, she gets my full attention from start to finish. I never rush."

Time to prove that to her. I lick my fingers and trace the wet tips down her thighs while I blow a gentle stream of air across her flesh in their wake. Avery sucks in a breath and grips the table's edges. I nuzzle her mound, pulling in a deep draft of her scent, and groan with appreciation. It's not an act. Everything about her gives me pleasure, even when I'm not shagging her. I keep my gaze on her face while I whisper my hot breath over her mound, then I comb my fingers through the hairs.

"Hugh," she moans, arching her neck. "Please."

I tease her folds with two fingers, skimming them up and down so slowly that she whimpers, then I lightly flick one fingernail over the head of her clitoris.

"Oh God," she cries out. "Don't think I can take much more."

"You can, and you will. Trust me, darling."

"I do trust you."

"Open your eyes and look at me, please."

She peels her lids apart, and our gazes meet.

I tease her clit with the side of my finger this time, and her whole body jerks. "I'm going to pet your soft, wet folds while I thrust my tongue inside you."

"Yes, please, yes."

"No need to beg, darling, but I love it when you do that."

As I stroke her inner folds with my fingers, I lower my head to her opening, exhaling heated breaths onto her sensitized flesh. Avery is breathing harder, and her cheeks are flushed. She has never looked more beautiful or more desirable.

I seal my lips over her entrance and thrust my tongue inside.

She bucks her hips and shouts my name.

And I devour her, lapping at her inner walls, thrusting deep, rubbing her nub all the while. She thrashes and grips the table even harder, her wild movements making the table thump. I feast on her cream, loving the sweetly addictive scent and flavor, until the first spasm of her release hits. Then I plunge two fingers inside her and pump until she finally goes limp.

I lift my head to appreciate the beauty of a thoroughly satisfied woman. "You are stunning, Avery. The way you look just after you come makes me need to fuck you again."

"Oh, Hugh, that was…" She waves a hand as if she's fanning her face. "You live up to your nickname, that's for sure."

I pat her thigh. "You need to recover. Go into the bedroom and get comfortable. I'll find us a decadent snack."

When she doesn't move, I grasp her hands and pull her into a sitting position. She kisses me sweetly, then dashes off to the bedroom.

Am I falling for Avery? Not sure. For now, all I can think about is feeding her so she'll have the energy for another go-round.

Chapter Fourteen

Avery

I'm just coming out of the bathroom when Hugh walks into the bedroom carrying a tray of goodies, including chocolate candies and éclairs. Every item he brought would get us both arrested by the health food police, but I don't care. The incredible experiences we shared in the living room make me need snacks that are as decadent as Hugh himself.

After what we just did, I finally understand why women call him Lord Steamy. I'd experienced a taste of that side of him when we kissed and when we had phone sex. But the full-on version of Lord Steamy... There's no comparison. It was more than hot sex. I've never felt that kind of intimacy before, like it meant more than two people getting it on.

Maybe I am falling for Hugh, a little bit. But I still don't know if we could ever work as a genuine couple. Faking it is one thing. Really getting involved with him would come with a slew of sticky issues. His family. His company. His scandal. My business. My frequent traveling. My brother. Why does everything have to be so complicated?

Hugh pulls back the covers and sets the tray of goodies on the bed. "Climb in, love. I mean to feed you."

"All of that looks yummy." I slap his ass when I walk past him to jump onto the bed. "But you are even yummier."

"Nothing tastes as good as you." He climbs onto the bed, settling in beside me. Then he moves the tray over his lap, picks up an éclair, and holds it to my lips. The custard inside it has leaked out just enough to make my mouth water. "Take a bite. Let the silky filling glide over your tongue."

I open my mouth, and he slides a bit of the éclair between my lips. I lick at the custard and moan, then bite off a chunk and chew it slowly, moaning again just to tease Hugh. "Your turn."

He bites off half of the éclair.

Once he finishes chewing, I lick the remnants of custard off his lips. Then I slide a hand down his inner thigh. "How long until you can fuck me again?"

"I'll need a bit longer." He hands me a chocolate candy. "Try a Sommerleigh caramel truffle. You should eat while I tell you the last of the pathetic tale of my time in Scotland and what came after."

"There's more? I thought I knew everything."

"Not quite. I needed a break before I shared the rest." He grabs another truffle and shoves the whole thing in his mouth, chewing it up before he speaks again. "It involves the Duke's wife."

"Oh. I won't yell at you for what you did with her, if that's what you're worried about."

"I know you won't." He lets his head fall back against the wall and shuts his eyes. "But I'm not proud of my behavior during or shortly after my stay in Scotland."

"Whatever you tell me, it won't change my opinion of you. I already know you're a good man who made mistakes." I tickle his lips with my fingers until he looks at me. "News flash. I make mistakes too. Everyone does."

He thrusts another candy into my mouth. "When I found out Callum had been secretly shagging Kate, I was furious he'd lied to me. But more than that, I was jealous. My anger toward Callum stemmed mostly from my envy of his relationship with the only woman I had ever wanted for more than sex. I did not behave well in the aftermath."

I grab a glass of water off his tray and guzzle it. "I won't judge you for whatever you did."

"Yes, I know." Hugh almost smirks, but the expression fizzles out. He picks up a napkin and wipes my mouth with it. "You have chocolate on your face."

"Oops. These treats taste so good that I can't control myself."

"Your utter lack of decorum is endearing." He drops the napkin on the tray, staring down at it. "I did a terrible thing. The MacTaggarts had arranged a series of games designed to help me and Callum realize we'd both been arses and needed to get over it. One of their ideas was to have us all play shinty—nude shinty."

"What is shinty?"

"A Scottish sport, something like lacrosse with the flavor of hockey. The MacTaggarts love shinty, and rules aren't really a part of their mindset. Intentionally injuring another player is the one of the few sins a bloke can commit on the shinty pitch. That's the field they play on." He takes a long swig from his glass of water. "I broke their only rule. I rammed into Callum on purpose and knocked him down."

"Was he injured?"

"No, not badly, thank heaven. I regretted what I'd done as soon as it happened. Callum was able to finish the game and win. After that, we talked through our issues and saved our friendship."

"So it all worked out."

He screws up his mouth as he stares down at the tray of treats. "Not long after that, I slunk back home to lick my wounds. Though Callum and I had saved our friendship, it hasn't been the same since."

Though I understand why he feels uncomfortable with the idea of talking to Callum, I also know he needs to deal with that problem instead of hiding from it. But I should hear the rest before I tell him that.

"After my humiliation in Scotland," he says, "I decided to hire a car and drive home instead of flying. Taking it slow seemed like the thing to do. On the last leg of my drive, I stopped at a pub to have a drink and, well, wallow in my guilt and shame. A bloody stupid thing to do, I know. But not as stupid as what I did next."

"You met Annabelle."

He nods. "She was already in the pub, and I sat down beside her at the bar because all the other stools were taken. We got to talking, and I...did what I usually do. I flirted with her. I didn't know who she was, and I thought she had no idea who I was. When she asked me to go upstairs to her room, I knew exactly what she wanted. In my condition, I had no business seducing a woman, even if she initiated it. But I thought I would never see her again."

"I'm confused. How did she know who you were?"

"Not sure, but I assume she rifled through my wallet. Things weren't in the same place in the morning, and my driving license was sticking out of it." He wipes a hand over his eyes, his lips warping into a slight frown. "Annabelle left me a note thanking 'Lord Steamy' for showing her a good time. And she signed the note as 'The Duchess of Wackenbourne' as if she wanted me to know I'd just made a monumental mistake. She wasn't wearing a wedding ring, but still…"

"That's horrible. She must've told her husband about you, right?"

"Yes, she did. I have no proof of that, but I'm sure it's what happened. After the things I've done lately, I deserve to be punished."

He thrusts an entire éclair into his mouth.

I wait until he finishes chewing, then I lay a palm on his cheek and force him to look at me. "You do not deserve to be punished. Making a mistake is not a capital offense, and Annabelle should've told you from the start who she was. The Duchess is the one who needs to atone for her actions."

"So do I. But if Sommerleigh Sweets falls, I will never forgive myself."

"You are not solely responsible for the scandal."

"I know, but I'd never done anything reckless in my life, not until that night in the pub." He closes his eyes and sighs. "Now one mistake might ruin my family and my employees."

"That won't happen." I touch my lips to his. "You've got me on your side, and I will not let a silly scandal ruin anything. Trust me, this is what I do. Whatever it takes, however long it takes, we will prove to the world that you are an upstanding citizen."

"Do you fight for all your clients this way?"

"In bed? No." I kiss him again. "You're a special case."

"You know what I meant. The way you're determined to save me seems to go above and beyond your job description." He winces. "Or maybe I'm being an arrogant arse, assuming you—"

I seal his lips with my fingers. "I've never cared this much about helping a client before. I do my job and do it well. But I like you more than I've ever liked anyone else, either clients or men I dated. This has become personal, and I need to do this for you."

"Pretend to date me. That's what you need to do."

"Yes." Maybe I want it to be more than that, but right now, we should both focus on fixing the problems that nasty duke has created. First, though, I need to convince Hugh to face up to his issues, starting with the most obvious one. "Do you have a date for Callum and Kate's wedding?"

"No. I was planning to go alone." He squirms and clears his throat. "Though since you are my fake girlfriend, maybe you wouldn't mind…"

"Yes, I'll be your date."

His entire posture relaxes visibly, and he gives me a grateful smile. "Thank you, Avery."

"No problem. It's my job."

"Before the wedding, though, I think I need to, ah…introduce you to my family."

"I've met your mom."

He stares at me for a moment. Then he hisses under his breath, "Bollocks. I forgot about that. How can you be my fake girlfriend when Mum hired you? This will never work."

"Since we've established ourselves as a couple, in public, it's too late to back out. Besides, I bet your mom will be thrilled. She likes me."

"But she paid you to be my image consultant, not to get involved with me."

"Chill out, Hugh. Everything will be fine."

He raises his brows. "Chill out? That's not a professional word."

"I'm naked in bed with you. This isn't the time to discuss business or to worry about what might happen tomorrow or the next day." I sneak my hand down to clasp his dick. "Let's see how fast you can get in the mood."

"Very fast." He sets the tray on the nightstand and pulls me onto his lap. "Can you feel how in the mood I am?"

Oh yes, I can feel that. His dick is already firming up.

He wraps his arms around me, burying his face against my neck. "When I'm with you, I know everything will work out."

After another round of Lord Steamy sex, we fall asleep while spooning. I wake up before Hugh does in the morning, but I can't make myself crawl out of bed just yet. No, I'm not ready to give up the feel of his warm body snuggled against mine and his breaths whispering over my neck. How far will I go to save Lord Sommerleigh and his company? I'll do whatever it takes. But for Hugh himself, I would go around the world and back again. *Oh shit.* I really do have feelings for him—strong feelings. That realization should probably scare me, but now that the initial shock has worn off, it doesn't bother me at all.

Still, I won't mention my feelings to him yet. He has enough to deal with right now.

Hugh stirs and rocks his hips into me. "Mm, good morning, darling."

"Good morning. How do you feel?"

"Brilliant. Like I could conquer the world."

I laugh and roll over to kiss him. "Let's start with conquering your scandal and go from there."

"Of course." He sits up and slaps my bottom. "Get up, love. It's time for a shower."

"Together?"

"Yes. I'll get the water running and heated up."

I watch Hugh slide off the bed and saunter into the bathroom. Damn, that man has a fine ass. Everything inch of him is beautiful and sexy and designed to drive a woman wild. By the time I amble into the bathroom, steam has already filled the open shower. But yeah, we generate some extra steam while getting clean. We laugh a lot too because Hugh Parrish has a surprisingly sweet and playful side that he hides from most people. I love that I get to see every facet of him, maybe even things his best friend doesn't know about him.

As we exit the bedroom, Hugh veers away to go into the kitchen and make breakfast for us. I plan to perch on a stool and watch him, but I hear my cell phone ringing. Where did I leave that thing? I remember walking into the flat, sitting in the armchair and then on the sofa, telling Hugh he's irresistible... Oh, I know where I left my phone.

I march over to the armchair and find my purse lying on the floor beside it. My phone is still ringing, but I need to answer quick before it goes to voice mail. The caller ID says, "Derek." My heart stutters, and my throat tightens, but I grab the phone and answer. Derek is calling to say hi, not to lambaste me for sleeping with Hugh. He doesn't know about that.

"Hey, sis," Derek says. "Where are you?"

"Why do you want to know?"

My brother chuckles. "Kinda touchy this morning, eh? Relax, I'm here to help."

"Help with what?" I freeze, and I swear every molecule in my body turns to ice. "What do you mean you're *here* to help?"

"Exactly what I said. I'm standing outside your hotel suite. But you don't answer, no matter how hard I bang on the door. The people in other rooms are probably going to call the cops any second."

"What?" I all but shriek as I whirl around to gape at empty space because I can't gape at my brother. Not yet. "Why are you in London?"

Hugh glances over his shoulder at me, his brows furrowed.

"Oh, hey," Derek says in the sneaky tone I know all too well. "Now that we're on the phone together, I can track you on the map thing-amajig. We set that up in case of emergency, remember? Be there in a jiff."

My brother hangs up on me.

What emergency? I'm sleeping with Hugh, not being held hostage.

Hugh rushes over, grasping my shoulders. "What's wrong, love? You look pale."

"Um, uh..." I squeeze my eyes shut, suddenly feeling like a naughty teenager. "My brother is in London, at my hotel. And he's coming here."

Chapter Fifteen

Hugh

*W*hy would your brother be coming to my flat?" I ask. Avery mentioned she has a brother and that he can be overbearing at times, but she failed to mention the bloke might fly to the UK to check up on her. Am I scared? No, of course not. But I would have appreciated a warning.

Avery bows her head and moans—pitifully, not in a sexy way. "Derek thinks he needs to protect me from you."

"From me? What have I ever done to the bloke?"

She raises her head to look straight at me. "He got online and saw the photos of us out on the town together. Then he read the articles about your scandal."

"Blimey. No wonder he wants to check on you." I glance at the clock in the kitchen. "Your hotel isn't that far from here. Depending on how quickly he can get a taxi, your brother might be here fairly soon."

Her eyes go wide. "Oh God, I'm wearing the same clothes as yesterday."

I cup her face in my hands. "Relax, darling. Your brother doesn't know that."

"Oh. Right." She hunches her shoulders and bites her bottom lip. "Sorry I freaked out. It's just that Derek has a habit of scaring away any guys I date that he doesn't like, just by showing up to glare at them."

I guide her over to the sofa, urging her to sit down, and rest my bum on the coffee table. "Don't worry about me. I'm not a weakling."

"You don't know my brother. He needs to be very tough to do his job."

"What sort of job does he have?"

"Derek is a bodyguard. And an amateur boxer. He's won eleven bouts."

He does sound quite tough. Still, if I can handle the MacTaggarts, this brother of hers won't frighten me. But Avery is panicking, which I haven't seen her do before. She must care what her brother thinks of her life choices, otherwise she wouldn't be in such a state. "Are you worried he won't approve of me? Or are you starting to regret what we did last night?"

"Neither. I've dated guys Derek didn't like. The ones who ran away weren't worth my time, anyway."

"I will not run. Don't care what Derek says or does."

She blinks rapidly, her eyes large, as she gazes at me. "You really aren't worried, are you?"

"No." I get up and wave for her to stay put when she starts to rise too. "Relax on the sofa, pet, while I make breakfast—for three."

I head for the kitchen, but something makes me pause at the bar to glance back at Avery. She sits on the sofa with her knees drawn up and her arms locked around them, seeming much younger and less like a businesswoman. Her casual blouse and jeans make her seem even more innocent. After what I did with her last night and this morning, I can't claim to be innocent myself. Am I corrupting her? No, Avery is a strong and confident woman who makes her own decisions. But a surprise visit from a family member can knock even the most mature person off balance.

I want to go over there and…just hold her.

But instead, I walk into the kitchen and start making breakfast. Avery needs comfort food now, so I decide on eggy bread and bacon. A dash of vanilla will improve the flavor and the smell of our food, so I add that to the mix. Just as I've finished cooking everything, the doorbell rings.

Avery flies off the sofa, spinning around to gawp at the door. "It's Derek."

"Yes, love, I'm sure it is." I walk out of the kitchen, heading for the door, but I hesitate halfway there to glance back at her. "Do you need a tranquilizer?"

"Oh God, yes."

I march over there, pull her into my arms, and kiss her.

The doorbell rings again.

When I pull away from her, she gazes at me with a slightly dazed expression. I kiss her forehead. "There. You're ready now."

I stride to the door and swing it open.

A muscular gent with massive biceps and eyes the same color as Avery's glowers at me. "You must be the British jackass who's making time with my baby sister."

"You must be the American lout who thinks his adult sister needs his protection." I hold out my hand. "Hugh Parrish, the Viscount Sommerleigh."

"Uh-huh." He glances at my hand, his lip curling. "Where's Avery?"

I give up and lower my arm. Then I hook a thumb over my shoulder. "Over there, in the living room."

Derek pushes past me, almost knocking me over, and stomps up to Avery. She now stands behind the sofa with her arms lashed around her.

I shut the door and join them. "Well, Derek, it's lovely to meet you at last."

"At last?" He snorts. "Yeah, I bet you were dying to meet me."

"Why not? I enjoy making new friends."

He laughs in a way that I'm sure he thinks is menacing, though it doesn't bother me. "Friends? I don't get chummy with British jackasses who seduce my baby sister."

"You said virtually the same thing a moment ago. Perhaps you should buy a thesaurus and expand your vocabulary."

Derek narrows his gaze and flexes those biceps. "It's more likely I'll use an unabridged dictionary to beat you senseless."

I scoff. "I've been kidnapped by a clan of angry Scots. You don't scare me."

He cracks his knuckles. "Maybe not. But I'll get a warm, fuzzy feeling from whupping your ass."

"Enough!" Avery shouts. She sets her mouth in a hard line and flicks her flinty gaze between me and her brother. "I am not a child, and I certainly don't need you two to fight over who makes decisions about my life. The answer is me. I'm the only one who runs my life. Got it?"

I want to drag her into the bedroom and fuck her. Nothing else gets me as randy as a strong woman asserting herself. Especially when that woman is Avery Hahn.

Derek and I turn our attention to her at the same time.

"No arguing," she says. "Got it? Derek, if you can't act like a normal human being, you can fly right back to New York. And Hugh, stop acting like an arrogant aristocrat."

Arrogant? Her brother deserves to be called that too, but I won't say so.

Derek relaxes all those bulging muscles and sighs. "Okay, okay. I'll put up with your new boyfriend for now."

"Thank you," Avery says. Then she turns to me. "Derek isn't actually an asshole. He's being overprotective."

"Yes, I gathered as much." I cast a sideways glance at her brother. "Threatening to beat me up was a slight clue."

Derek lifts his chin and sniffs the air. "Something smells good. Did you guys eat already? The meal on the plane tasted like warmed-over garbage."

I clap a hand on his shoulder. "Don't worry. I've made a proper breakfast for the three of us."

"What kind of breakfast?"

"Eggy bread."

Derek's lip curls again, and he draws his head back. "That sounds like something a chicken would barf up."

"He means French toast," Avery explains. "I've been to England often enough to know what they call things. Most of the time."

I wink at her. "I'm sure I could stump you if I tried."

"Mm-hm. I'm sure you could."

"Hey!" Derek snaps. "No flirting with my sister in front of me."

I raise my brows at him. "So, you don't mind if I flirt with her in private."

When he opens his mouth to speak, Avery raises one finger and gives him that flinty look again.

Derek throws his hands up in surrender.

"Mind eating at the bar?" I ask. "Or would you prefer the official dining table?"

"Bar's fine with me." His mouth curves into a mischievous smile. "Does it come with booze? I'm still on Eastern time, which means it's happy hour."

Avery punches his arm. "No, that means it's after closing time."

She might be younger than her much larger and less cuddly brother, but Avery does not let that stop her from putting Derek in his place. I love that about her.

The siblings take seats at the bar.

I bring the food out of the oven, where I'd kept it warm, and set a plate down in front of each of them. "Careful. These plates are hot."

"Just the way I like them," Derek says. He rubs his palms together. "Damn, this smells good."

Avery takes a bite of her eggy bread, and her eyes roll back in her head as she moans. "Hugh, this is incredible."

Derek moves his hand as if he means to take her plate away. "Maybe you shouldn't eat that. Lord Sticky must've dumped pheromones on yours."

"It's Lord Steamy," I say. "Not Lord Sticky."

"Oh yeah, that really makes it all better."

"Why don't you try my food before you condemn it?"

He takes a bite and chews it slowly while wearing a thoughtful expression. "Not half bad. But you Brits need to change what you call your foods. Americans know how to think up names that sound appealing instead of like something a rat wouldn't touch."

Derek wants to annoy me, but I ignore his comment and grab my plate, then sit down beside Avery.

She slides a hand down to my inner thigh. "This really is a yummy breakfast. You're an amazing cook."

Derek is staring at my leg with his lips puckered and his eyes narrowed.

I delicately remove Avery's hand from my thigh. Not because Derek frightens me. He doesn't. But I don't care to infuriate him any further because I can tell Avery loves her brother. She will want us to get on, which means I need to rein in my, ah, usual instincts.

Honestly, I've never needed to worry about a girl's brother before. After all the women I've shagged, it seems amazing that this issue hasn't come up. Maybe that's because I've never wanted more than sex with anyone—until recently. I want that more than ever with Avery.

Derek Hahn will not chase me away.

"I thought Avery and I would visit Sommerleigh today," I tell Derek. "Would you care to come along?"

"What is Sommerleigh?"

"My family's ancestral home. I am Lord Sommerleigh."

"Thought you were Lord Steamy."

"I'm both."

Derek spears a piece of eggy bread. "Uh-*huh*."

Chewing a mouthful of food gives me a chance to gauge Avery's reaction to what I suggested. She gazes at me with... No, it can't be that. I misunderstood her expression. But when she leans in and kisses my cheek, I know I was right. She *is* gazing at me with adoration.

And I think I might be giving her the same look.

"What do you say, Derek?" I ask. "Would you like to meet my mother?"

"Absolutely."

"I'm afraid my cousins won't join us today, but you could meet them another time if you like."

"Sure, why not. They can't be any smarmier than you."

"It's called charm, not smarm. Though I can see how that might've confused you since the last three letters are the same."

"Might want to dial back the sarcasm." He aims a sneaky smile at me. "You'll be stuck in a car with me for...how long?"

Bugger me. I forgot about that. "Two and a half hours."

He chuckles and slaps my back—four times. "We'll get to know each other really well, won't we? Either that or your mommy will kiss a corpse hello."

Derek Hahn is beginning to remind me of the MacTaggarts. They love gallows humor too.

After breakfast, we climb into my car. Derek needs to sit in front with me, the driver, since he claims he can't fit in the backseat of my four-door Jaguar. Well, he might have a point. I never ride in the backseat, so I can't promise he wouldn't be uncomfortable back there. I've never had more than one passenger until today.

When we stop to get petrol a little while later, Derek goes inside the store to use the restroom and Avery gets out to stretch her legs, as she says. That means she goes into the store to buy sweets and beverages. When she offers me a bottle of lemonade, I ask if she's comfortable in the backseat.

"Sure, I'm fine," she says. "But thank you for asking. It was very gentlemanly of you to let my brother sit up front."

"Gentlemanly? No, I just didn't want his laser eyes to burn a hole through the back of my head."

She laughs and kisses my cheek. "You are so adorably sweet."

"If you're expecting me to balk at being called sweet and adorable, you'll be disappointed. I know that to a woman those words are a high compliment."

We get back on the road a few minutes later, and every time I glance in the rearview mirror, Avery is smiling at me with what I can only characterize as affection. I experience a strange flush of warmth in my chest when I see that expression on her face. Yes, all right, maybe I am falling for her. But after the disaster in Scotland, I'm not sure I can trust what I think I see or feel.

Derek tunes the radio to country western music. Bagpipes would be better than that, but I let him have his way—to be polite, that's all.

Half an hour from Sommerleigh, I can't resist asking a question. First, I turn down the volume on the radio and wait for the whining twang in my ears to subside. "Derek, I'm curious. Avery said you're a bodyguard, and I'm wondering what sort of clients you have. Wealthy people, I assume."

"Oh yeah, it's rich people. Normal folks can't afford a full-time bodyguard. But I can't tell you the names of my clients."

"No, of course not. Do you work for a company?"

"I own the company. Started out as an employee and took over as owner after my boss retired."

"That's impressive."

Despite the close quarters, Derek manages to bend one leg to the side to hook his ankle over the other knee. "So tell me, Lord Sticky, how's your business doing? I read stuff about you online, and it sounds like your company's about to get flushed down the toilet."

I'd hoped to avoid thinking about my problems for one day. But no, of course I can't do that. Because Derek is right. I am single-handedly flushing my company down the toilet. "Yes, the business is in trouble. But with Avery's help, I'm hopeful we can turn things around."

Unless the Duke of Wackenbourne brings out his big gun—the House of Lords.

Chapter Sixteen

Avery

"Stop harassing Hugh," I tell my brother. "You know damn well his title is Lord Sommerleigh, not Lord Sticky. And Hugh is going through a rough time right now, but he's a smart and capable man who will figure out a solution."

My brother twists in his seat to look at me. "You really like this guy, don't you?"

"Yes, I do. So be nice, Derek."

He salutes me, smirks, and faces forward again.

In the rearview mirror, I can see Hugh. His eyes are wide, and he's staring at me. I suppose I shouldn't have admitted I really like him, but I've never been comfortable with lying or evading the truth.

"What's the deal with that duke?" my brother asks Hugh. "He's got an iron hard-on for you. Seems like it must be more than the fact you slept with his wife."

I jab a finger into Derek's arm. "Cut it out."

He raises his hands. "Okay, okay, I'll shut up."

"We're almost there," Hugh says. "You will meet my mother, Lady Sommerleigh, and I'd appreciate it if you referred to her by her title."

"Sure, no problem," Derek says. "I'm always nice to the ladies."

I poke his arm again. "I know you're polite to women, but please respect the etiquette of the British aristocracy."

"Like you know all about that. Come on, you got that stuff from your new boyfriend."

"Just promise you'll behave."

He twists around to look at me again. "I promise, Avery. Happy now?"

"Yes. Thank you."

I don't know why I worry so much about how Derek will behave when he meets Hugh's mom. I guess I'm just worried Lady Sommerleigh won't approve of me dating her son, since she hired me to help Hugh. I've suffered only a twinge of guilt about that so far, but I'm about to meet his mother again under very different circumstances than the first time. Yes, I have anxiety. For heaven's sake, I've dealt with some of the most powerful people on earth and didn't flinch no matter what they said or did. If I can stand in front of an audience of international journalists to deliver a press conference, I can handle Lady Sommerleigh. She seemed very nice during our one and only meeting.

But I wasn't sleeping with her son back then.

We turn down a long gravel driveway. I can't even see the house from here, thanks to the woods that surround Sommerleigh. We roll down, down, down the driveway that seems like it will never end, and I realize I've started wringing my hands. *Get a grip, woman, right now.*

"Here we are," Hugh says as we finally exit the woods. "Welcome to Sommerleigh House."

I've never been here before since Lady Sommerleigh had met me at my hotel in London the only time we spoke in person. Sommerleigh House isn't as huge as other mansions I've seen, though the three-story mansion has a typical English-style boxy shape. Elegant decorative elements soften the hard edges. I see a pair of stone lions perched at either side of the steps that lead down to the circular drive.

Hugh parks right in front of those steps. He and Derek climb out of the car, but I remain paralyzed in the backseat until Hugh opens the door and offers me his hand. I stare at it like I've never seen a hand before because I suddenly can't remember anything, not even my own name.

Okay, the amnesia only lasts for about three seconds. Then I remember who I am.

"Come, love," Hugh says. "Unless you plan to eat and sleep in the backseat of my car."

"No, I don't want to do that." I take his hand as I hop out. "Guess I'm more nervous than I realized."

"You've met Mum before."

"I know. But it feels different now."

"Why? I won't tell anyone we've shagged."

"But your mom will know." I bite one side of my lip. "Moms always know. And I guess I'm worried about what she'll think of me now that we are sleeping together."

His lips kink into a playful smirk. "*Are* sleeping together? That implies you want to go on doing that."

"Yes, I do. You don't?"

"Of course I want that. I want you, full stop."

I experience the most bizarre urge to giggle, but I quash it. A mature, professional woman doesn't laugh like a little girl just because the man she likes admits he feels the same way.

He glances down at our linked hands. "Would you rather we not hold hands when we walk into the house?"

"No, I don't want to hide our relationship."

"Even if it means Mum figures out it's no longer a fake relationship?"

"Yes, Hugh, even if."

He grins. "Brilliant!"

I can't help it. I grin too, just like a silly schoolgirl.

Hugh and I lead the way up the wide stone steps, past the guardian lions, straight to the double doors that form the entrance. Hugh doesn't knock. Well, duh, it's his house. He pushes one half of the doors open and walks right in.

A butler rushes toward us. "Sir, I was waiting for you to ring the bell."

Hugh halts near the poor butler, who seems frazzled by Lord Sommerleigh's abrupt arrival. "Relax, Kendall. This is hardly the first time I've entered the house without ringing the bell."

"No, sir, but it is the first time you've brought guests."

Hugh has never invited anyone to his home? I'll need to ask him about that later, when we're alone.

"Kendall, meet Derek and Avery Hahn," Hugh says. "Derek is Avery's brother, and she's my...girlfriend."

Hugh glances at me as if he's not sure whether he should've said that. I smile to let him know I'm fine with it.

"Girlfriend?" Kendall says. He breaks into a wide grin. "That's wonderful, sir."

My boyfriend averts his gaze and scratches his neck. Not sure if he's uneasy because he just declared I'm his girlfriend or if it's because the butler keeps calling him "sir." Since the day I met Hugh, I've gotten the impression his title and the deference it grants him make him uncomfortable.

"Where is Mum?" Hugh asks.

Kendall turns sideways to us, spreading an arm as if inviting us to go first. "Lady Sommerleigh is in the solarium. Shall I announce you?"

"You know how I feel about all that propriety rubbish. Mum will be shocked if I let you announce me."

"Of course, sir."

Hugh guides us down a long hallway to a room at the end and pushes the door open. Derek follows us into the cozy yet elegant room known as the solarium. Since I've visited other English mansions before, I knew what this room was before Hugh opened the door. It's a glass-enclosed porch with furniture appropriate for such a space, things like outdoor chaises and rattan chairs with puffy cushions.

Lady Sommerleigh sits on one of those chairs near the windows, but she leaps up when we enter the room. The elegant and ever-ladylike mother of the viscount rushes over to hug her son and kiss his cheek. "Hugh, darling, I'm so glad you've come home."

His brows lift slightly. "Yes, Mum, I'm glad too."

Lady Sommerleigh clasps my free hand since Hugh still holds onto the other one. She glances down at our intertwined fingers, then smiles at me. "I'm not at all surprised that my son has fallen in love with you, Avery. You're precisely the sort of woman he needs."

"We're not in love," Hugh tells his mother in a surprisingly level tone. "We're dating. Let's not jump to conclusions."

"Of course not. But women realize these things long before men do."

I haven't realized what she hopes I have. I like Hugh a lot, and I'm his girlfriend. That's all.

Kendall pokes his head through the door. "Lunch will be served in ten minutes."

"We shall be on time," Lady Sommerleigh says. "Parrishes are never late. But first, I need to meet this gentleman my son has brought with him."

Hugh moves aside so his mom can see Derek, who had been loitering behind us. "Mum, this is Derek Hahn, Avery's brother."

She rushes toward Derek and clasps his hand while beaming at him. "What a pleasure it is to meet you, my dear. Avery is such a lovely woman that I'm sure you must be an equally lovely man." She rakes her gaze over his body. "You certainly have a beautiful face and physique. Do you like older women?"

"Mum!" Hugh snaps. "Honestly, what happened to decorum and all that properness rubbish?"

"Oh, tosh." Lady Sommerleigh waves a dismissive hand. "I'm in my own home with my family—and new friends. I can tease this beautiful man you've brought home. Do you work with your sister, Mr. Hahn?"

"No, I'm a bodyguard."

"Derek owns his own company," I say. "He's a very impressive man."

"I can see that," Lady Sommerleigh says. She hooks her arm around Derek's. "You will sit beside me at lunch. We need to get better acquainted—'we' meaning you, Avery, and I."

"That would be terrific," Derek tells her. "Hugh and I got to know each other in the car. Didn't we, Lord Sommerleigh?"

Naturally, my brother invokes Hugh's title in a sarcastic tone.

"Oh, we certainly did that," Hugh agrees with equal sarcasm. "Derek and I are best mates now."

Lady Sommerleigh gives her son a motherly smile. "I'm so happy you've made friends at last. I adore Callum, but he lives far away. You need local friends too."

"Are you going to Callum's wedding, Lady Sommerleigh?" I ask. "Hugh invited me to be his date."

"My son is attending Callum's wedding?" she says. "I wasn't aware the lovely boy was engaged. Hugh, why didn't you tell me?"

"Because I, ah, wasn't sure I wanted to go."

"Of course you do." She eyes her son up and down, and her brows draw together. "What's wrong, dear? Did you and Callum have an argument?"

Hugh glances out the window and winces. "It's complicated, Mum. But I've agreed to serve as Callum's best man, and Avery has agreed to be my date. You can come too, if you like."

"Yes, I would love that."

Lady Sommerleigh still seems confused, but being a proper Englishwoman, she hides that fact very well. "My, but I am famished. I'm sure Mildred has cooked up a delicious midday feast for us."

We all follow Lady Sommerleigh down the hall and into the dining room, where a feast really does await us. Do British aristocrats always eat this much for lunch? Or have they made a special Sunday meal for us? I don't think Hugh has come home for a while, so maybe his mother wants to celebrate the fact he's here now.

Hugh sits at the head of the table, but his mother insists on sitting beside me. When her son points out that's not proper, she says "tosh" and does it anyway. Derek winds up on the other side of the table, seated kitty-corner to Hugh. We all chat during lunch, mostly about mundane things. Derek tells Lady Sommerleigh stories about his adventures as a bodyguard, and she laughs heartily at every humorous moment he relates.

Lady Sommerleigh is not at all what I expected, based on previous conversations. During our video calls and our one in-person meeting, she had behaved with all the grace and decorum I expected from a woman of her station. But I like finding out she's not always that way. Hugh does not care about being proper, though he would never intentionally embarrass his family. And I love that about him.

After lunch, Lady Sommerleigh asks me to take a walk in the garden with her. Hugh defers to his mom and suggests he'll take Derek on a tour of the garage. When my brother seems dubious about what a great privilege that is, Hugh informs him that the Sommerleigh garage is "nothing to sneeze at, mate." Apparently, it's enormous.

We ladies amble out into the gorgeous garden that occupies most of the open area behind the house. Colorful flowers bloom on bushes and in ground beds, while a small maze takes up one corner of the garden. Lady Sommerleigh leads me to a concrete bench nestled under an arbor.

"I adore you, Avery," she says as she takes my hand. "And Hugh adores you even more. I'm delighted that you two have fallen in love. I know Hugh won't admit to that yet, but you and I can be honest with each other. Can't we?"

"Yes. But I'm not sure what I feel for Hugh, not yet."

"Trust an old woman's intuition." She enfolds my hand with both of hers. "You are the perfect one for Hugh, and he's the right one for you too."

My cheeks grow warm, and my heart beats faster. "Hugh means a lot to me, Lady Sommerleigh. But I need more time to figure out if we could have a future together."

"Please call me Rosalyn. I know my son, and he has never looked at any other woman the way he looks at you."

I swallow, but my throat remains dry and tight.

"Hugh has believed for a long time that he never wants to marry," Rosalyn says. "But I always knew he would change his mind when the right woman came along. I imagine you've seen sides of him I haven't, and that's as it should be."

"I care about him, really I do. But my job takes me all over the world, and Hugh seems like a homebody."

Her lips curve into a soft smile. "You might be surprised by what each of you is willing to do for the other. Love can change your world."

I open my mouth but can't produce any words.

She rises and gestures for me to do the same. "Now, let's explore the garden. Then we'll find the boys."

As I follow her down a gravel path lined with gorgeous flowers, I can't stop myself from wondering. Can Hugh and I merge our lives? Or is our relationship destined to fail?

Chapter Seventeen

Hugh

*Y*ou've got some awesome rides," Derek says as he wanders through the garage to examine each of the twelve vehicles housed inside the building. "But I don't see any American cars. They're much more reliable than these British and German ones."

"Well, you would say that. You are American, after all." I lean my thigh against the bonnet of the Mercedes Derek is currently inspecting. "You're prejudiced against everything British, including me."

"No, I love British football and your mom."

"If you try to date my mother, I will run you over with my Jaguar."

"Is that your car or your pet cat?" He turns toward me, shoving his hands into his trouser pockets. "I'm not excited about you dating my sister, so we're even."

"You think I'm a useless chancer."

"Maybe I'd agree with that statement if I knew what it meant."

"A chancer is a person who cares only about his own desires and needs."

Derek studies me for a moment, his gaze narrowed. Then he sighs and shrugs. "No, I don't think you're like that. Avery wouldn't be so into you if that were true."

She's "into" me? Well, I'm into her too, literally and figuratively, though the literal version happens only when we're alone.

"When are you taking my sister to Scotland?" he asks. "I'd like to spend more time with her."

I weigh my options, and Avery's happiness wins out. "The wedding is on Saturday. I'm sure I could get you an invite if you'd like."

"Yeah, I'd love that. Never been to Scotland—or England, actually, until now."

"Maybe you'll meet a bonnie lass there. I know several MacTaggart women who are available. That's the clan my mate Callum belongs to."

"I don't need any help getting dates, Lord Sticky. Do just fine on my own. But I'd love to see Scotland."

"How can I convince you to call me Hugh instead of Lord Sticky?"

"Can't." Derek claps a hand on my shoulder. "This is what happens when you date somebody's baby sister. Get used to the harassment."

As we leave the garage, the driveway comes into view with my car still parked there.

"Gotta admit," Derek says. "Your Jag is pretty cool."

"Care to take it for a test drive?"

"Seriously? Yeah, that would be amazing. Riding in the Jag isn't the same."

I drape an arm around his shoulders and offer him the Jaguar key. "A car is like a woman. She responds to a delicate touch much better than sheer power. Treat her right, and she will do anything for you."

"Hmm. Is that how you seduced my sister? Doesn't work on me." He snatches the key from my fingers. "But I'll take you up on that test drive."

"I think I should come along. Can't have you getting lost."

"All right. But I'm in charge. Don't wanna hear any sound come out of your mouth unless you're screaming that we're about to crash into a tree."

"So, crashing in the river would be acceptable."

He shrugs away from my arm. "You really are one snarky jackass."

"Yes. But Avery loves that about me." I bar my arms over my chest. "Better get used to it since your sister is my girlfriend."

"Why do you think I'm sticking around?" He holds two fingers to his face, indicating his eyes, then rotates those fingers toward me. "I'm watching you."

I follow Derek to the Jaguar and give him a brief lesson on how to handle a high-end sports car. He rolls his eyes but doesn't insult me or make any snide comments. Then he starts up the engine and revs it so loudly that the noise echoes off the house. Fortunately, he only does that for a few seconds.

"Are you trying to destroy my car?" I ask. "Because I happen to know several excellent solicitors who would happily sue you on my behalf."

"Not scared, asswipe. I know lawyers too." He shuts the driver's door, then rolls the window down to give me a self-satisfied smile. "The guy I'm working for now is the best attorney in the good ol' US of A. We're tight. That means we're close friends."

"Yes, I know what 'tight' means."

I get in on the passenger side, which feels odd since I always drive this car. I've never been the one sitting in the seat watching. Derek eases his foot off the brake pedal and steers the car around the circular drive at a speed so slow that I know he's having me on.

"Do all Americans drive like decrepit old women?" I ask. "The American blokes I know wouldn't be caught dead driving a sports car at a snail's pace. I suppose you're afraid of what British engineering can do."

"Oh, you're asking for it now."

He floors the accelerator, and the car rockets forward. I'm pinned to my seat briefly, but that does not frighten me. Whether Derek hoped to scare me, I have no idea. He whirls round and round the circular drive until he finally stops—by slamming on the brakes. Gravel sprays up, cracking on the exterior.

"Damn," he says. "This is a great ride you've got."

"What's left of it. You've probably burnt out the brakes and left pockmarks all over it."

"Nah." He throws the door open and climbs out, stretching and groaning. "If this car can't handle pea gravel, it's not much of a vehicle."

I get out and warily inspect the car, walking all the way round it. "Well, at least you didn't damage anything."

For the rest of the afternoon, we all decide to spend time having fun together. Mum suggests we sit outside at the table on the outdoor patio, which lies right next to the solarium windows. That doesn't surprise me since Mum loves to be outside, but her next suggestion shocks me.

"Let's play games," she announces. "We have cards as well as board games."

My jaw must've dropped because I feel a draft tickling my tongue. "Are you serious? We haven't done that since before..."

"Your father passed away. Yes, I know that." She hooks her arm around Derek's as we traverse the solarium, heading for the outdoor patio. "But it's been almost a decade since your father's passing, and I shouldn't have let us go so long without reigniting our passion for games."

"We used to have a lot of fun, didn't we?"

"Indeed we did. And now we shall again."

Avery and I collect the games from the wooden chest in the solarium and bring the lot outside where Mum and Derek are already laughing. I've come to terms with the fact Lady Sommerleigh has a motherly crush on my girlfriend's brother. I can understand it. He is charming in his American way, and he treats Mum with respect. He also loves his sister and would do anything to protect her. That's another quality I admire.

I would do anything for Avery too, because I love her.

The realization hits me so hard that I stumble, but I catch myself before I tumble to the ground. Avery gives me a strange look and asks if I'm all right. I tell her yes, which is sort of a lie. I'm not all right. I feel bloody fantastic, and though I want to share my epiphany with her, I need to wait until we're alone and preferably naked.

For the next three hours, we play games. Kendall brings us refreshments and snacks on a regular basis, as any dedicated butler would. He's also an honorary member of the family, like all our employees are. Kendall also inquires whether the ladies would like a blanket, but they say no. It is a warm and sunny day, after all. Kendall sets up a large umbrella that fits into a slot at the center of the patio table, providing shade for the four of us.

That man deserves a raise. An obscenely large one.

By the time Kendall reminds us dinner will be served in half an hour, Derek has beaten me at Scrabble twice. Well, he beat all of us, not only me. Avery's brother also trounces me at three other board games, as well as poker. It does not wound my ego to lose to an American. I'm not that sensitive. But after dinner, I pretend to feel grievously wounded.

"Want me to make you feel better?" she asks while we climb the stairs to the second floor on our way to my bedroom. "I mean, Derek did beat the pants off you. Let me soothe your bruises with my mouth, my tongue, my fingers, and any other part of my body you want."

"Oh yes, I absolutely need that sort of consolation. Your brother has destroyed my sense of self-worth."

She pokes me with her elbow. "I know you're teasing me. You like Derek, and he likes you."

"That's true. Does this mean I don't get that consoling session?"

"Of course you do."

When we walk into my bedroom, Avery halts abruptly. Her face goes blank. Only her eyes move as she takes in the expansive space with its posh furniture and posh decor.

"Holy cow," she says at last. "This is bigger than my condo back in New York."

"I doubt that."

"This is really where you sleep whenever you're home."

"Yes. This is the viscount's bedroom. My parents slept here until Dad passed away, then I was forced to move in here. Tried to convince Mum she should keep this room, but she wouldn't hear of it. 'This is the viscount's quarters, and you are the Viscount Sommerleigh now.' That's what she said."

"Rosalyn cares about what's proper. I admire her dedication to following tradition." Avery glances around the room, her eyes lighting up. "Mind if I try out the bed?"

"Go ahead. You'll be sleeping on it tonight."

She grins and belly flops onto the bed, then rolls side to side while giggling.

I have never heard her laugh that way before, and I love it. But I can't resist jumping onto the bed feet first, which makes the whole thing jostle wildly. Then I lie down beside her. We both roll over at the same time so we're facing each other.

Avery nudges me with her knee. "You mother told me you'll turn thirty in two months. She wants to have a big party for you."

"Party? That's overkill." I eye her with curiosity. "I want to ask how old you are, but I can't."

"Why not?"

"Because it would be ungentlemanly."

She kisses me, then taps a finger on my nose. "You are so sweet, Hugh. But I'm not sensitive about my age. I'm thirty-two."

"An older woman? I've shagged several of those, but I've never dated one."

"I've never dated a younger man."

"How can that be? You're beautiful, sexy, clever, and accomplished. Blokes should be queuing up to beg for a chance to date you."

She smiles with such tenderness that I get another of those odd sensations in my chest. "Most men are intimidated by accomplished women. They feel inadequate or jealous or...whatever."

"Those wankers must be insane."

Avery snuggles up to me, and our noses rub against each other. "That's why I love you."

"Why, exactly? I'm confused."

"Because you think successful women are hot."

Avery slides off the bed, heading for the bathroom. She smiles over her shoulder at me as she asks, "Mind if I take a shower?"

"Have at it, darling."

Only after she goes into the bathroom do I realize what she said a moment ago. *That's why I love you.* The statement could have been an offhanded remark. She might not mean she genuinely loves me. But I love her, and I need to tell her that right now.

So I strip off my clothes and join her in the shower.

Avery startles when I open the frosted glass door, but her surprise quickly melts into a sensual smile.

"Mind if I help you get clean?" I ask. "It will involve getting dirty first."

"I'd love to do that." She loops her arms around my neck. "Showering with you is the best kind of dirty."

"First, there's something I need to tell you." I back her up to the tile wall, pressing my growing erection into her belly. "I love you, Avery."

She grins. "I love you too, Lord Steamy."

"Care to know a secret?"

"Absolutely."

I push her feet apart. "I love it when you call me Lord Steamy."

"As much as you love me calling you by your given name?"

"No. When you whisper my name, I get so randy I can hardly breathe."

She shifts her arms down to wrap them around my waist. Her voice drops to a husky murmur as she plasters her mouth to my ear. "Let's get dirty, Hugh."

I rub my cock into her cleft. Then I realize something. "Oh, bollocks. I don't have a condom."

"Are you telling me Lord Steamy doesn't have a stash in his bathroom?"

"I've never shagged a woman in my bathroom or my bedroom."

She draws her head back and squints at me. "You must be joking."

"Afraid not. I never brought women here because this is my family's home, and none of my lovers meant more to me than a fling. The longest time I've spent with one woman has been these weeks with you."

"That's... Wow, I don't know what to say."

I grab a bottle of shampoo. "Well, if we're not getting dirty, then we might as well get clean."

"Are you telling me Lord Steamy can't think of a way to fuck me in the shower without a condom?"

Of course I can. Why am I acting like penetrative sex is the only way to get off? My confession made me feel uncomfortable. That's my only excuse.

I set the bottle on the shelf again and kneel before Avery. "Let me show you what Lord Steamy can do. Spread your thighs a bit more, love."

When she does that, I lift one of her legs to rest her knee on my shoulder.

And I show her exactly what I can do in the shower.

Chapter Eighteen

Avery

I moan as Hugh pushes his face between my thighs and latches on to my clitoris. His cheeks rub against my folds, and his breaths tickle the hairs down there, but he keeps his gaze locked on mine. I thrust my fingers into his hair while I struggle to control my uneven breathing, but I finally give up and let myself gasp and pant and moan. His tongue torments my nub, and I know any second I'll come.

He withdraws his head and licks his lips, groaning with intense satisfaction.

"Why did you stop?" I ask, and I don't care that I sound breathless and desperate. "Please, Hugh, make me come."

"I will, darling. But not yet." He rises and skims his gaze over my entire body. "Face the wall."

"What?"

"Face the wall. I promise you won't regret it."

When I turn around, he clasps my wrists to raise my hands and press my hands to the wall. Then he sets his own palms on the tiles beside mine. His chin rests on my shoulder. "You want to know what I can do without penetration?"

"Oh, yes. Show me, Hugh."

He pushes my legs even wider apart and thrusts his cock between my legs, gliding it along my cleft, up and down, up and down, while

I grow slicker and hotter and more tingly every second. I instinctively rock my hips into his movements, and when I glance down, I can see the rosy tip of his erection poking out between my folds. The harder he thrusts, the more I hear his balls slapping against my ass.

I throw my head back and moan so deeply that I can't believe I made that sound.

Hugh spreads a hand over my throat and nips my earlobe. When I suck his finger into my mouth, he groans and moves his hand down to palm my breast. "Head down, Avery. Watch me fucking you with my cock and my hand."

I follow his orders because I love everything he does to me and I want him to command me—if only when we're having sex. He doesn't want to order me around the rest of the time, which is one of the reasons I love him.

So I bow my head and watch.

Hugh pinches my nipple, making me gasp. Then he slides his palm down my belly to slip two fingers between my folds. He begins to rub my clit and stroke my outer folds while maintaining the pace of the powerful strokes of his cock. I whimper and moan and gasp, my fingers crooking and my nails scraping on the tile wall.

"Oh God, Hugh, yes!"

"Ready to come, aren't you?" he says, his voice rough and strained.

"Please, yes, make me come."

He plunges his cock inside me and massages my nub harder.

The orgasm explodes through me while my muscles clench his length over and over, and he keeps pounding into me, eliciting a wet sucking sound. I squeeze my eyes shut and cry out so many times that my throat hurts and I can't breathe anymore.

Hugh pulls out and just stands there with his erection nestled between my folds. "Open your eyes and watch me come."

I peel my lids apart and look down. The tip of his cock just barely peeks out.

He plants his palms on the wall and starts pumping. His grunts and groans echo in the bathroom as his pace accelerates until, finally, he lets out a guttural shout. Milky liquid jets out of his cock. He pumps again, twice, then he slumps against me. His chin touches my shoulder. "Did I live up to your expectations?"

"Definitely."

"Glad to hear it." He steps back and slaps my bottom. "Now that we've gotten dirty, it's time to clean up."

After our official shower, the one that involves getting clean, we go back into the bedroom. But someone knocks on the door.

Hugh pulls on a robe and suggests I hide under the covers while he marches over to the door and opens it a few inches. "Mum? What is it?"

"Will you and your guests be staying the night?"

"Not sure." He glances back at me. "Do you want to spend the night and leave early in the morning? Or would you rather we drive home now?"

"Probably best if we leave now. Don't want you to be late for work when you're in the middle of trying to convince everyone you're a trustworthy businessman."

"Right." He turns back to the door. "We'll be leaving soon. Please let Derek know."

"Of course. I'll wait for you in the foyer, so we can say goodbye."

He shuts the door.

We both get dressed and head down to the foyer, where Rosalyn and Derek are waiting for us. Kendall is there too, standing near the door—to open it for us, no doubt. He seems like a relatively young man, but he has all the composure and competence of a seasoned butler.

Rosalyn kisses both my cheeks and gives me a quick hug.

Hugh's brows lift. Then his mother pulls him in for a firm hug, and his eyes go wide as if he's shocked. She'd hugged him when we arrived, and he seemed surprised then, but this is a more boisterous embrace. She kisses his cheek and says, "Have a safe drive back to London. I hope you'll come home more often now, my darling boy."

Next, she hugs and kisses Derek.

Once the three of us get into the car—with Hugh driving, naturally—I want to ask him why he seemed shocked when his mother hugged him. But I don't get the chance.

My brother clears his throat. "Guess your mom doesn't hug you much, huh, Hugh? You got that deer-in-the-headlights look when she grabbed you."

"We Parrishes aren't known for hugging. When my father died, none of us even cried—in public. Can't say if Mum did that in private."

"Did you cry?" I ask.

"Not in front of anyone." He grimaces slightly. "But in private, yes. Not often, though."

"There's no shame in crying. You lost your dad."

"She's right," Derek says. "Everybody cries over stuff like that. And I think your mom wants to be more, uh, demonstrative with you."

Hugh jerks his head to glance at my brother. "What makes you say that?"

"Because I had a nice talk with her while you were defiling my sister in your den of debauchery." He lays a hand on Hugh's shoulder. "That means your bedroom."

"Yes, I figured that out." Hugh faces forward again but still seems a touch disturbed by Derek's revelation. "I would love to know what Mum said to you, but your conversation was private."

"I don't think she'd mind. Rosalyn's a great lady."

Hugh fidgets as he guides the Jag out onto the main road. "What did Mum tell you?"

"That she loves you a lot and she only wants you to be happy. Then she talked about how she wished she and your dad hadn't been so concerned with propriety and had hugged you more. In private, they were very affectionate with each other."

"If you're about to tell me about my parents' sex life, please don't."

Derek chuckles. "No, it's nothing like that. They liked to snuggle in bed together and talk. They always kissed each other good night too."

"I can't believe my mother told you all of that. She must really like you—and trust you."

"Not stealing your mom. I think it was easier for her to talk to me about that stuff since I'm not her son. I bet she'll tell you everything, eventually." Derek pauses, then asks, "Hey, is Rosalyn coming to the wedding?"

"Callum's wedding?" Hugh says. "Yes, she is."

"Has she met those Scots before?"

"Only Callum and his brother, Jack."

Hugh turns on the radio and plays it louder than he had on our journey to Sommerleigh. I think he's confused and wants to avoid hearing any other revelations about his mom. I can understand why she might prefer to tell those things to Derek. She likes him, and he's easy to talk to—plus, she probably guessed my brother would tell Hugh everything. That might be her way of testing the waters. If Hugh doesn't panic when Derek shares the details, she might assume that means he can cope with hearing more.

It's dark when we reach London, and I suggest Derek should spend the night in my hotel suite while I stay at Hugh's place. My brother doesn't argue, so we drop him off at the hotel. By the time we walk into Hugh's flat, we're both so exhausted we want nothing more than to sleep. Shedding our clothes depletes the last of our energy, and we snuggle under the covers to drift off.

When morning comes, we drive to Hugh's office. Derek had told us he would go sightseeing today, alone, but that he'd like to have dinner with us tonight. Hugh offered to treat my brother to a gourmet meal at a restaurant, which seemed like the perfect way to continue our campaign to convince everyone that Lord Sommerleigh is an upstanding citizen. If they see us with my brother, it will prove our relationship is genuine.

But for now, we need to deal with repairing the image of Hugh's company so we can save it from a hard and fast downfall. We've just sat down in his office, with Hugh behind the desk and me sitting across from him.

I tap one finger on my leather portfolio. "I think you should call Phillip Jenkins. He's had plenty of time to think, and you need to show initiative. After the weekend we had, I hope you're feeling refreshed and confident."

Hugh straightens in his chair. "I was feeling that way until you suggested I should ring Jenkins."

"Ever heard the phrase 'rip off the Band-Aid'?"

"Yes."

"Do that now, Hugh. No point in torturing yourself any longer."

He rubs his forehead and sighs. "Yes, I know you're right."

Just as he reaches for his desk phone, it rings.

"It's Trudy," he says, then he picks up the handset. "Yes? Oh, please do."

"Everything okay?" I whisper.

He holds his hand over the speaker. "Jenkins just rang the office, and Trudy is transferring the call."

I suddenly realize I'm tapping my finger faster and drumming my shoes on the floor. Though I force myself to stop those nervous gestures and maintain a calm demeanor, I can't do anything to quell my anxiety. Jenkins will stay with Sommerleigh Sweets, right? He won't end a longstanding business relationship because of what one duke said.

"Good morning, Mr. Jenkins," Hugh says in a bright tone that doesn't match his tense expression. He listens and nods, making the appropriate noises, but he looks more anxious with every passing second. Finally, he bows his head. "Yes, I understand. It's not your fault. I appreciate that you informed me personally, and I'm grateful our companies had such a long and fruitful partnership."

Hugh hangs up. Then he slumps in his chair and shuts his eyes, letting out a long sigh that deflates him even more.

"I take it that didn't go well."

"No." He picks up a pen and twirls it around his finger, then he flings it across the room. "We've lost Jenkins Foods."

"I'm so sorry, Hugh. But you have two other distributors, right?"

"Yes." He leans forward to rest his arms on the desk and stares down at the surface. "One company distributes our products on the Scottish mainland. The other handles the islands."

"Sounds like that won't sustain Sommerleigh Sweets."

"No. We will suffer a slow and painful death."

Can we really do nothing else to save the company? There must be another way. We need to try anything and everything to stop the Duke of Wackenbourne from hammering the last nail into the coffin of Sommerleigh Sweets.

Hugh straightens and adjusts his tie. "I need to write a statement that I will deliver to our employees in person. We'll hold a company-wide staff meeting on the production floor as soon as we can get everyone here."

"That's a good idea, but don't focus on the negative news. Let your people know you're fighting for them and for the company. They need to feel you haven't given up."

"Haven't I done that? I'd be lying to them."

"No, you wouldn't." I walk behind his desk and perch on its edge. "Be honest, but also be hopeful. I know you think all is lost, but we can turn this around together."

"I appreciate having you as my cheerleader, but I can't—"

"Shush." I place two fingers over his mouth. "Listen to what I'm about to say. Really listen. Okay?"

He nods.

I remove my fingers. "You're a viscount and a businessman. Use your connections to get people on your side. You and I will do this together. We both need to start calling people, and keep calling until we get laryngitis. Everyone in the UK can't be against you. We also need to plan some special events to continue repairing your public image."

"That sounds incredibly time-consuming and exhausting, not to mention bloody pointless."

"It's not pointless." I set my hands on his chair's arms and rotate it toward me, then slant in until our faces are inches apart. "I'm not giving up on you, and I will not let you give up on yourself. Understand?"

He stares at me for a moment, then his mouth spreads into a sexy grin. "You're wonderful, Avery. I'd love to shag you right now."

"We can do that later. First, it's time to make those phone calls."

And that's what we do for the rest of the day and all week too. We dial phone numbers until our fingers start to ache and then we keep going anyway. Nobody wants to risk doing business with us, but I still don't understand why. The Duke of Wackenbourne isn't a high-powered politician, and as far as I can tell, nobody paid much attention to him until Hugh slept with his wife. Not even the members of the House of Lords seemed to care much about him. Once the Duke triggered that stupid scandal, suddenly Hugh became a celebrity of the worst sort—and everyone got to know Benedict Pemberton-Rice.

But we aren't giving up yet.

Chapter Nineteen

Hugh

*A*very Hahn truly is an amazing woman. She refuses to give up, no matter how heavily the odds are stacked against us. I no longer think of my problems as only *my* problems. Avery insists we're doing this together, and I won't argue the point. The mess I've become embroiled in affects us both, and we will deal with it as a couple. If she ever needed my help, I would crawl across a field of broken glass while naked and blindfolded if that would spare her even a small measure of pain.

She insists I am not allowed to give up, not until we have scoured every last corner of the globe. Despite our Herculean efforts, we lose the last two distributors. No one in the world can buy our merchandise until we find someone, anyone, who isn't afraid of the Duke of Wackenbourne. Maybe I should ring Kirsty MacTaggart and ask the self-professed Wiccan to cast a curse on Benedict Pemberton-Rice. Couldn't hurt, right?

But I don't do that. Instead, on Wednesday afternoon, I go to the factory floor and stand on a makeshift dais constructed from wooden boxes and give my speech. Avery helped me write it. Honestly, I could never get through any of this without her. Mum might have hired Avery to save my reputation, but she unknowingly gave me a gift that changed my life.

At the end of my speech, the entire staff of Sommerleigh Sweets erupts in cheers and clapping and whistling. Then they begin to chant, "We love Hugh." I've always told my employees they can call me Hugh, but I never imagined they would do that with so much enthusiasm. Their boisterous show of support gets me choked up, and tears gather in my eyes. I don't cry, though. I wipe away the wetness and square my shoulders, then walk into the crowd to thank each and every employee, shaking so many hands that my fingers ache. Women kiss my cheek and hug me. Blokes hug me too, but they don't kiss my cheek.

One gent, a gray-haired man, clasps my hand firmly and doesn't let go. "Your speech was brilliant, Lord Sommerleigh. I loved that part at the end about adversity. You reminded me of Winston Churchill right then."

The gent finally releases my hand, then thumps me on the back.

What had I said at the end? My speech has become a blur, especially after greeting every employee afterward. But yes, I think I know which bit he meant.

Adversity cannot destroy our spirit, for we are more than a collection of employees and executives. We are a family. Whatever might befall us, nothing can shatter the courage and dedication of every person who helped make this company a success. I might be the viscount and the CEO, but we are all Sommerleigh.

That was when the cacophony erupted. I'm not sure that speech compares to anything Winston Churchill had delivered, but I'll accept the compliment.

Now, if we can only save the company...

Derek has been exploring London while his sister and I toil to prevent the company from disintegrating, but to my utter shock, I see him among the employees on the factory floor. Avery had stood beside me during my speech, and I'd been too anxious to notice every face in the crowd. Now, he saunters up to me and...pulls me into a quick hug.

Then he slaps my arm. "Good job, Your Highness."

"A viscount is never referred to as 'Your Highness.' Just call me Hugh."

"You gave a terrific speech."

"Thank you, but Avery contributed a great deal."

"I'm sure she did. But you got up there and said all of that without tripping over even one syllable. I'm impressed. You aren't just a pretty face, Lord Sticky."

Nothing short of a heavenly visitation will convince Derek to stop calling me that. Harassment is a form of affection between men, especially the Americans and the Scots.

Now that we've informed the employees of the current dilemma, Avery announces we need to get moving on repairing my reputation. She arranges for Lord Sommerleigh to host a charity gala for a children's hospital. Should I worry that I just referred to myself in my thoughts as "Lord Sommerleigh"? If I've developed a narcissistic streak, eradicating that will need to wait awhile.

Avery thinks I'm being "adorably silly" when I tell her I worry that I've become an egomaniac.

"Your confidence is coming back," she says. "That's a good sign. Don't beat yourself up anymore."

Since I can't deny Avery anything she wants, I do what she told me. I stop worrying and admit, to her and to myself, that regaining my confidence is a positive sign. I'd been mired in self-loathing for too long, thanks to my failed attempt to woo Kate Wagner as well as my mistake with the Duchess, which still threatens to ruin my company.

But we will fix things. Avery swears we will, and I trust her completely.

We attend two social events this week, but the first one couldn't compare to the charity gala Avery organized for the children's hospital. It was magnificent and raised a shedload of money, but we have more pressing matters to deal with over the weekend. On Friday afternoon, we all climb aboard a jet sent by Evan MacTaggart that will ferry us to the Scottish Highlands. The entourage includes me and Avery, of course, but also Derek and my mother. Mum spends most of the flight chatting to Derek, which leaves me alone with my girlfriend. Of course, "alone" means we sit at the opposite end of the cabin. We aren't literally by ourselves. And I'm grateful for that.

Once we land at Inverness, I feel the old anxiety creeping back into me. Why? Oh, nothing much. I'm about to walk into a horde of Scots, but that doesn't bother me. What "fashes" me, as the Scots would say, is seeing Callum and Kate again. I don't pine for her. But I hadn't behaved in the most gentlemanly way the last time I saw them. And yes, I've avoided all my mates ever since.

Avery slips her hand into mine as we trudge down the stairs and step onto the tarmac. Derek and Mum are just exiting the jet. Nearby, a limousine awaits.

The limo door swings open, and Callum jumps out to race toward me.

Bloody hell. I hoped I'd have more time before I saw him. More time? To do what? I have no ruddy idea.

Avery gives my hand a light squeeze and whispers, "You can do this."

Callum drags me into a bear hug and thumps me on the back so hard that I feel like a bass drum. Avery's hand is torn away from mine. I glance at her and see she's grinning. When Callum finally releases me and takes a step back, he grins too.

"Feel like I havenae seen ye in years," he says. "I hear you've been hiding in your London flat because of the scunner who calls himself a duke."

"Not hiding. I retired from the public eye momentarily."

"But you're back now, eh? And ye brought your lass." Callum seizes Avery and hugs her as fiercely as he'd done to me. "Welcome to Scotland. I'm Callum MacTaggart."

"Avery Hahn. I've heard a lot about you."

"You're Hugh's lass, aye? About bloody time he settled down."

Kate comes up beside Callum and nudges him in the side with her elbow. "You better not be sexually harassing Hugh's girlfriend."

"I hugged her. It's called being friendly, *mo leannan*. Unless you'd rather I growl at the lass."

"Do you want me to start calling you Pig-Bear? I'm sure Piper wouldn't mind if I borrow her nickname for Magnus."

They're teasing each other. Do Avery and I do that? I think so, but we don't use Gaelic words. "*Mo leannan*" means "my sweetheart." Would Avery like it if I whispered to her in Gaelic? No, that would make me a copycat. I can think of original ways to tell her how much I love her.

Avery leans in and murmurs, "Pig-Bear?"

"I'm not sure what that's about. Magnus is Callum's cousin, but I don't know about Piper."

Callum chuckles. "We can hear you two whispering. Piper is Magnus's fiancée. They met when she became a fugitive, accused of murder, and Magnus the bounty hunter went after her. She was innocent, of course. Pig-Bear is the nickname Piper gave to Magnus because he often grunts and growls like a pig or a bear."

Avery seems confused. I can't blame her. Pig-Bear? That must be the most ridiculous name these people have ever invented. It's even worse than when Derek refers to me as Lord Sticky.

Mum and Derek have just reached the tarmac. My mother throws her arms around Callum and kisses his cheek repeatedly. "I'm so happy you and Hugh have patched things up."

"Patched what up?" Callum says. "We were never torn apart. Just a wee bit frazzled, that's all."

He's being extremely kind in his assessment of what happened the last time I came to Scotland.

I introduce Derek to Callum and Kate, and they hit it off immediately. Well, he can be charming in his "I'd murder you in a heartbeat if you hurt my sister" way. Since I never want to hurt Avery, her brother won't find any excuses for dispatching me. I admire Derek's determination to protect his sister. I admire the way the Mac-Taggarts stick together too, though they are a bit like a Scottish mafia. Even one of their own, Callum's cousin Iain, describes them that way. But the MacTaggart mafia only intervenes to ensure good people get what they deserve.

We all stroll toward the limo, and the others pile into the car. But Callum ushers me around to the other side where I see a familiar object.

I raise one brow at Callum. "Why are you showing me your Harley? How did you even get your motorcycle here?"

He laughs and pats my shoulder. "How do ye think? I drove it here."

As my American mates would say, "duh." Perhaps I should slap my palm on my forehead when I think that pseudo-word. "You want to ride your Harley all the way back to Loch Fairbairn? It's a three-hour drive."

His smile turns disconcertingly smug. "Aye, but we won't be heading straight for Dùndubhan. You and I need to get reacquainted."

"Your brother the psychologist suggested that, I imagine."

"No, it was Kate's idea." He waves to the driver through the limo's front window, and the vehicle rolls across the tarmac away from us. "She's a clever lass, and she wants us to be best mates again. And before ye complain that we already are, she meant that we need to spend time alone together."

"What sort of humiliating male-bonding ritual do you have in mind? I refuse to dance naked by the light of a bonfire."

"Ye think I want to see ye naked again?" He scoffs. "Once was enough. Get on the bike, Hugh. This is the last phase of your therapy, as ordered by Kate who knows what she's doing."

Because she is both a physical therapist and a psychotherapist. I wouldn't balk at this plan except for one issue. "You expect me to ride on your motorcycle with my arms around you and our bodies...touching."

"That's how you ride a bike, mate."

It seems I need one more round of humiliation before Callum will forgive me for knocking him down during the shinty match. I deserve it. "Fine, give me a helmet."

He reaches into the plastic storage box situated at the rear of the motorcycle and hands me a helmet.

I roll my eyes and raise the thing. "It's pink, Callum."

"Aye, that's Kate's helmet. She lent it to you."

Thank you so much, Kate Wagner.

Callum squints at me in a sarcastic manner. "You better not be cursing at my fiancée in your head."

"No, I was cursing at you. What is that lovely phrase you like to say? Oh, yes. Flying vagina, you are a plague."

"It sounds better in Gaelic." He climbs astride the Harley. "Get on, Hugh."

"You know I hate this machine."

"Aye, ye told me all about that during the radical intervention." He starts up the engine and puts his helmet on, then shouts, "Hurry up, Lord Sommerleigh."

He needed to shout because this bloody monstrosity roars like a dragon. But I dutifully don my pink helmet and get on the Harley, then latch my arms around Callum's midsection. And we roar across the tarmac. Soon, we're racing down the highway. We pass the limo, and Callum and I wave to the ladies and Derek as we leave them in our wake. During our first hour on the road, we stop twice so that I can, as Callum puts it, rest my "erse" and my "*bagais.*" Yes, my balls do need a break from the vibrating engine.

An hour and fifteen minutes after our journey began, Callum turns off onto a side road. Not long after that, he turns down a gravel road the width of a single car where trees form a canopy above our heads. Eventually the forest opens to reveal a clearing around a small house. Callum parks near the porch steps and shuts off the Harley's engine. We both slide off the bike and remove our helmets.

"What is this place?" I ask.

"One of my mates from the fire station owns this cabin. He's letting us use it for the night."

"Aren't you missing your rehearsal dinner?"

"No. Kate and I decided not to have one. Instead, I'm spending time with my best mate."

I have no idea how to respond to that. He gave up going to a do with his family so we could repair our friendship.

When I follow him into the cabin, I get a surprise. The exterior looks like it could use a bit of TLC, but inside, the house is quite cozy and comfortable. Someone took the time to clean up the place and furnish it. One piece of furniture in particular grabs my attention.

"That's quite a table," I say. "Live edge is all the rage, isn't it?"

"Aye. I made that table, and a similar one that's in my house in Loch Fairbairn. Kate loves all my furniture."

Callum starts a fire, and the two of us sit down to watch the flames.

"Is this all that male bonding consists of?" I ask. "Have to say I'm rather disappointed. Shouldn't we beat each other up or something?"

"Donnae worry. This is only the beginning." He leans toward me, his gaze nailed to mine. "We have big plans for you, Lord Sommerleigh."

Chapter Twenty

Avery

I spent the night in an honest-to-goodness castle. Kate Wagner had taken me under her wing and showed me around Dùndubhan, which is both a stark, boxy medieval relic and a beautiful, elegant environment. Part of the castle is a museum, but it's closed for the weekend. Callum and Kate's wedding will take place here, on the grassy area behind Dùndubhan. Kate told me it's called "the green."

Even though Callum sort of shanghaied Hugh, I slept very well last night. Hugh needs to spend time with his best friend so they can reforge their bond. A night alone with Callum will seal the deal, Kate tells me. Since she's a psychologist, I believe her.

The next morning, I eat breakfast with several MacTaggarts, and some Brits too including Hugh's friends the Dixons and the Hunters. We eat alfresco in the gorgeous walled garden, then everyone heads out onto the green to finish setting everything up for the wedding this afternoon. Though Kate tells me I don't need to help, I assure her I'm happy to pitch in. The bride disappears through the garden, heading back to the castle proper so she can get ready for her wedding.

A woman I met at breakfast—Emery, wife of Rory MacTaggart—puts me to work arranging chairs for the ceremony and putting name tags on them. Everyone will have an assigned seat. I'm not slaving away alone, though. I meet a group of people who tell me they're "naturists," aka nudists, and they all work at a naturist resort in Oregon. Wow, I can honestly say I've never met nudists before. They seem like wonderful people.

We've just finished setting up the chairs, and I'm standing behind the rows to admire the beautiful altar and the wedding arch that's overflowing with flower garlands.

Hands cover my eyes. Not my hands.

"I have a surprise for you, darling," Hugh says. "Are you ready?"

"Yes."

He removes his hands, then I hear a rustling sound right before he steps in front of me. Hugh is holding a garment bag slung over his shoulder. "I thought you should have something new to wear for the wedding and the ceilidh after."

"The what after?"

"Ceilidh. It's essentially a Scottish party with drinks and dancing—a particular sort of dancing. I can teach you the basics."

"Sounds like fun." I wrap my arms around his neck and kiss him. "Missed you last night."

"I missed you too, love." He kisses me, but then his brows wrinkle. "Where's Mum?"

"Still inside the castle getting ready, I guess."

He hands me the garment bag. "You will look even more stunning than usual in this dress."

"Thank you for buying it for me." I take the bag and drape it over the nearest chair. "How did your male bonding go? Lots of drum beating and howling like wolves?"

"No. We sat in the living room of a cabin owned by Callum's mate at the fire station and talked while enjoying a crackling fire and a bottle of Scotch."

"That's not what I expected."

"I share your confusion." He slips an arm around my waist and grabs the garment bag as we amble toward the castle compound. "I expected something outlandish since that is the MacTaggart way. But we just chatted to each other for hours. I feel much better this morning, and I think that's because I finally know for sure that Callum and I are still my best mates."

"Don't think Callum ever doubted that."

"No, I was the arse who thought I needed to hide from everyone who cares about me. I'm done with that now." He leads me through the open door to the garden but stops us halfway across the flower-covered space. "Whatever happens, I know I can get through it—because of you."

"I provided moral support. You did the rest."

"Bollocks. You did much more than that." He lifts my hand to his lips and kisses the knuckles one by one. "You saved my soul, Avery. Even if I can't save the company, I'll know it wasn't my fault because I did everything I could to save it. Somehow, I will help my employees find jobs elsewhere."

"We'll do it together."

Hugh takes me out of the garden and across the courtyard to the doorway I know leads into the vestibule of the castle proper. At the bottom of the spiral staircase, we say goodbye. Hugh has best man duties to perform.

"I'm curious," I say. "Doesn't Callum's brother feel slighted? You're the best man instead of Jack."

"No, Jack understands. In fact, Callum told me last night that his brother insisted I should be best man since I'm the groom's best mate."

"I can see why you love these people. They're amazing."

"Have you met the gang from the Au Naturel Naturist Resort?"

"Yes, I have. They're lots of fun. I met the Wiccan sisters too. Is there brother really a former spy?"

"Oh, yes. Logan MacTaggart was in the army, then MI6. Now he's a security consultant for the company owned by his cousin Evan who's a billionaire."

"I know. I met Evan and his wife, Keely, earlier this morning. Their daughter is adorable."

Hugh shuffles over to the staircase but hesitates there, glancing back at me. "Would you ever want children? With me?"

"Of course I would. I love you."

The cutest little smile curls his lips. "I'd want that too, because I'm in love with you."

He starts up the stairs.

I watch until he disappears through a doorway high above my head. When Lady Sommerleigh hired me, I could never have imagined how meeting my newest client would change my life. I still don't know how to reconcile my vagabond career with Hugh's well-rooted lifestyle, but I know we can figure it out.

On my way to my room on the ground floor, I bump into Derek in the dining room. I need to cross through that space to reach the guest wing.

My brother grins at me. "You look flushed, Avery. Hugh must be back."

"I'm not flushed." My cheeks do feel a touch warm, but that is not the same thing. "Did you have fun with the Dixons and Hunters last night? I heard you guys played poker in the sitting room."

"Yeah. And I beat the socks off those Brits."

"Hugh knows all about your skill with cards and board games."

Derek's grin melts into a softer expression, and he clasps my hand. "If you want to marry Hugh, I'm good with that. Want my baby sister to be happy."

"I love Hugh, but it's too early to think about marriage." Though Hugh did ask if I'd like to have children with him, so maybe it's not too soon after all.

"Don't wait on my account. If he asks, promise me you'll say yes."

"Now you're ordering me to marry Hugh?"

Derek chuckles. "No, Avery. I'm giving you both my blessing."

I study my brother for a moment. "Did you meet a girl here? That would explain your sudden desire to get me hitched. Love makes people want everyone to be as happy as they are."

"Most of the women here are already married. Besides, I live in New York."

"So do I. That didn't stop me from getting involved with Hugh."

Now it's Derek's turn to study me. "Are you planning to move to the UK? Or does Hugh want to live in America?"

"We haven't talked about that yet."

He grasps my upper arms and gazes at me with such earnestness that my throat goes thick. "I want you to be happy. If that means you stay in the UK, I'm fine with that. Don't make any decisions based on where I live. Promise me that, okay?"

"I promise."

My brother kisses my forehead and walks out of the room.

The morning has raced by so fast that I didn't realize it's almost noon. The ceremony will begin at one o'clock. I rush to my room and unzip the garment bag. A warm, tingly feeling sweeps through me when I see what Hugh has chosen for me. It's a designer dress. Hugh chose a semi-formal one that will go with the tone of the wedding and the reception. The knee-length dress features a floral pattern on a powder-blue background. When I put the dress on, it fits just right.

Well, Hugh has explored my body thoroughly.

As I'm exiting the dining room into the ground-floor hallway, I see the bride in the vestibule. Several women hover around her to make minute adjustments to her ensemble. Kate wears a gorgeous wedding gown decorated with lace, bead work, and a small train. Her veil hangs behind her head in a cascade of lace that matches her dress.

Kate notices me standing outside the vestibule door and smiles. Then she winks. "I'll see you at the reception, Avery. Can't wait for your wedding."

I decide not to point out Hugh and I aren't even engaged yet. This is Kate's big day, and saying inappropriate things is the bride's prerogative.

Since Hugh is a member of the wedding party, I walk out onto the green alone. But I'm not alone for long. A man who tells me he's Errol Murdoch, Callum's cousin, offers to walk me to my assigned seat in the front row. He kisses my hand, then leaves. I'm sitting sandwiched between Callum's parents and Rosalyn Parrish, with Jack's pregnant wife on the other side of Greer and Alistair. Derek sits beside Rosalyn. Lady Sommerleigh wears a designer dress too, but hers is a tasteful silver number that covers her arms and extends partway down her calves. I wonder briefly if Hugh chose her outfit when he bought mine, but then I realize Rosalyn must have a closet full of haute couture. She doesn't need her son to buy her clothes.

I shift my attention to the altar—and my heart skips a beat.

Hugh stands between Callum and Jack wearing a kilt and a waist-length black jacket that has silver buttons and accents. He has a black bow tie too. A silver clip secures the length of plaid that drapes over his shoulder and down his back to halfway down his thigh. White socks cover his calves, and his shiny black shoes have laces that wind up his ankles. The kilt features a pattern that I assume is the MacTaggart clan tartan—light blue and green criscrossed with black and orange lines.

Hugh looks incredible in that outfit. He might not be Scottish, but damn, he should wear a kilt every day.

Music starts up, with a string quartet providing the ambiance as the two bridesmaids amble up the aisle to the altar. I recognize those two women, but I can't remember their names. Finally, the wedding march begins, and Kate walks down the aisle with her father.

My eyes tear up now and then, but I don't cry during the ceremony like most of the other women in attendance do. It's a beautiful event, and Kate and Callum's love for each other feels like a palpable force radiating through the crowd. Even the people who don't cry, like me, still seem as affected by this moment as I am.

Callum kisses his bride.

The crowd erupts with cheers, joyful shouts, and a deafening amount of clapping.

Hugh grins and slaps his friend on the back. Then he kisses the bride's cheek.

Kate turns around and hollers, "Ladies! If you're not married, get in position."

A horde of women scramble to line up in the aisle, but I stay put.

Kate raises her bouquet, readying for the traditional moment when someone will receive a floral sign of nuptials to come. Not that I believe a random toss decides anyone's fate. Kate glances over her shoulder, her smile so big and exuberant that it makes me beam too. Then she winks and tosses the bouquet.

It lands on my lap.

My entire body jerks like I've had a grenade dropped onto me. But when I glance at Hugh, he's grinning again. Now that the initial shock has faded, I pick up the bouquet and rise to wave it around for everyone to see.

The crowd cheers.

A bunch of flowers doesn't mean Hugh and I are getting married. He hasn't even asked me.

Callum scoops Kate up in his arms and carries her back down the aisle amid more cheers and whoops.

I wait while the guests gradually exit the green and head into the castle compound where the reception will take place in the great hall. Hugh loiters near the altar until I finally step out onto the beautiful red carpet that formed the aisle, then we walk hand in hand back to the castle. The reception is fantastic, but all I really want to do is cuddle up under the covers with Hugh and sleep.

When I wake up in the morning, sprawled across Hugh's body, my gaze drifts to the bridal bouquet on the nightstand. And I realize something important.

If Hugh asked me to marry him, I'd say yes.

Callum and Kate left last night for their honeymoon on a Caribbean island, absconding while the reception raged on in the great hall. The island is owned by a reclusive British author who became friends with Richard Hunter, one of Hugh's "mates" who owns a publishing company. Maybe someday we'll we get an invite to that island.

Hugh and I, as well as Jack and his wife, saw the happy couple off in the courtyard. Callum's cousin Evan provided the limousine that ferried them to the airport, the same car that brought me and Hugh and our entourage to Dùndubhan. Hugh unabashedly got choked up when he said goodbye to Callum, and I did too. Any vestiges of Hugh's issues with Callum and Kate have evaporated, and he assures me it's because of the past few weeks with me.

"I know that whatever happens now," he says, "it will not be my fault."

He means it. The conviction in his voice proves that.

"You know I'm here for you in whatever way you need," I tell him. "Hugs, advice, moral support, sex, anything."

"I love the way you slipped sex into that heartfelt declaration."

"With you, I always need to slip sex into the mix. You are Lord Steamy, after all."

He pulls me close. "I've come to appreciate that silly nickname since you started calling me that."

We join other wedding guests in the dining room for breakfast. The conversation is boisterous and results in plenty of laughter. But after the meal, Hugh and I are escorted into Rory MacTaggart's office here in the castle, along with several other men from the MacTaggart, Dixon, and Hunter families. They've all come up with some kind of plan, though no one has given us a clue yet about what they're plotting.

As we sit down on chairs positioned in front of Rory's desk, Hugh leans over to whisper into my ear, "I get nervous when these blokes insert themselves into my life, but only because not long ago they abducted me—for a good cause, and I'm genuinely grateful for their interference. If they hadn't held me hostage, I might never have realized how vacant my life had become. I certainly wouldn't have been worthy of a woman like you."

"You honestly are the sweetest man alive."

"I hope I'm the sexiest too."

"That goes without saying."

He kisses my cheek, and I might be blushing now.

"If you two are done snogging," says Richard Hunter, "we should get down to business."

Hugh lodges one ankle on the opposite knee. "Whatever you gents want to tell me, you will have my rapt attention."

"Good. Because this plan will make your abduction seem like child's play."

Chapter Twenty-One

Hugh

Rory MacTaggart occupies the chair behind the massive desk, but the others sit on the window seat, lean against the walls, or stand in various positions. This doesn't feel like the day when this lot had kidnapped me, though. It's much more serious.

"We've been thinking about you," Rory says as he leans forward to rest his arms on the desktop. "Been thinking a lot. You need help, and we are ready to provide it."

"I appreciate that, but I don't see how you can help."

Rory chuckles. "Ye still donnae get it, do ye? You have three families on your side, and a vast pool of talent to tap into whenever you need it."

"This is all a bit vague. Did you have something specific in mind?"

"Oh, aye." Rory glances at Chance Dixon, who leans against the wall beside the window seat where his two brothers sit. "Why don't you explain? This was your idea."

"It was a group effort," Chance says. "Hugh, we've developed a strategy. Avery has a handle on your public image. We mean to save your company and get that bloody duke off your back for good."

"Brilliant. How exactly do you mean to do that?" Yes, I'm less than convinced. But I know these men, and I'm fully aware of their skills and connections. Maybe they can save Sommerleigh Sweets. I don't know, but I have nothing to lose by letting them try.

Evan MacTaggart, who had loitered in the corner leaning against the bookshelves, ambles over to his cousin's desk. "I have more money than all my cousins and these Brits combined. Over the years, I've cultivated relationships with many people who are in a position to help."

"Do you have a particular someone in mind?"

"Aye. A fellow billionaire who is both an angel investor and the CEO of a business incubator."

"Sorry. Business incu-what?"

"Incubator. That's a company committed to helping other businesses succeed." Evan rests his arse on the corner of the desk. "With your permission, I'd like to contact this person on your behalf. Would you be open to that?"

"Yes, of course. If you think your contact might help, I'll try anything. It won't be long before I have to start letting my employees go." Something occurs to me, and I have to ask, "What about Celeste Arnaud? She's a billionaire, and her granddaughter is married to Reese Dixon. Might Celeste help?"

"We thought of that, but this isn't her kind of business deal. She's a cosmetics tycoon."

Reese raises his hand. "I'd be happy to ask Celeste. She loves me."

"Let's try my contact first," Evan says. "While you were busy shagging your wife last night, the rest of us discussed Hugh's problems. The person I have in mind could be even better than Celeste."

Reese shrugs and relaxes against the window seat.

Evan glances at Rory, who nods to Chance Dixon. "Your turn."

Chance folds his arms over his chest. "Rory and I have devised a legal scheme to convince the Duke to give up his vendetta."

"How?" I ask. "He wants me dead—figuratively, I hope—but dead, nonetheless. So I repeat, how do you mean to talk him out of that?"

"Lawsuits, of course. Elena and I have already spoken to the Duchess, via video call. She seems rather eager to save you."

Reese chuckles. "Must've been one bloody great shag, eh? Guess Hugh deserves his nickname."

I ignore him and focus on Chance. "No offense, mate, but isn't your wife a paralegal, not a lawyer?"

"Yes. But Elena has the keenest legal mind I've ever come across. We're the perfect team."

"Donnae forget about Stephen Beckham at the Home Office," Rory says. "He's on board too for anything we might need."

Logan MacTaggart steps out of a shadowy corner in true secret agent fashion. "I'll leverage my contacts in the covert world too. The Duke is going down, laddie. Going down hard."

When I glance at Avery, she's grinning.

I arch my brows. "What's so amusing?"

"Your friends should star in their own spy movie. This is like *Mission: Impossible.*"

To the Scots and Brits in the room, I say, "Forgive her. She's American."

Avery kicks my shin, though not hard. "Hey! This American helped save your British butt."

"That you did." I lean toward her until my lips graze her ear. Then I speak in a hushed tone only she will hear. "I'll show my appreciation, multiple times, when we're alone."

Chance clears his throat. "Getting back to the plan. You and Avery should go home to London and await further instructions."

Avery grins again. "See? Just like *Mission: Impossible.*"

We thank our mates, the men determined to save me, and then we climb into a limo for the drive back to the Inverness airport. By the time we walk into my flat in London, it's late afternoon. We ate lunch on the plane—yes, Evan's jet has a chef—so we aren't hungry. But I have something to say once we've settled onto the sofa together.

I clasp her hands. "Avery, will you marry me?"

She yawns and gives me a lopsided smile that's no less sexy for its lack of finesse. "Yes, Hugh, I would love to marry you."

"Even if my company goes bankrupt and I remain fodder for the tabloids?"

"Yes, even if."

Mum will not be Lady Sommerleigh for much longer, but I know she won't mind if it means having a daughter-in-law and the prospect of babies.

I raise a brow. "You yawned when I proposed. Maybe you should have a lie-down."

"Sorry about that. I got sleepy on the jet. Guess I finally relaxed after all the craziness lately."

Avery takes a nap while I make an early dinner for us. Then we stay up late just talking, but when we get up in the morning, we both feel refreshed. I suppose love will do that to a person. Can't swear to that since I've never been in love before. Avery offers to make breakfast, and I discover she is a brilliant chef. We've just finished cleaning up after our meal when the doorbell rings.

Avery rushes over to see who's out there. We both assume it's Derek. He stayed in Avery's hotel suite last night.

"Uh, Hugh?" Avery calls out to me. "Might want to come over here."

The tone of her voice spurs me to hurry over to her. And I freeze.

The woman standing just past the threshold bites her bottom lip and hunches her shoulders. "Hello, Hugh."

"Duchess," I say, and just manage not to stutter.

"We don't need to be formal. You called me Annabelle when we…knew each other before."

Yes, in the biblical sense. I don't really know her as a person. "What are you doing here?"

"I came to apologize, and to let you know I will do everything I can to foil my husband's attempts to make you a pariah."

"Well, I think it's a bit late for that."

"No, it isn't." She lifts her chin and rolls her shoulders back, seeming every bit the Duchess. "Benedict will do as I say if he means to keep me as his wife. You see, I hold all the money in our relationship. He might have been born a duke, but his wastrel family lost their fortune thanks to their habits of gambling, drinking, and whoring. All the money Benedict and I have came from my family—from me."

"Are you staying with him?" Not that it matters, but I can't deny I'm curious.

"Yes, I will stay with Benedict. I'm an aristocrat through and through, and I wish to remain the Duchess of Wackenbourne. You may not understand that, but this is how I was brought up. Duty before happiness."

My family raised me to value honor and kindness. But I understand what she's saying. Staying a duchess matters more to her than anything else. I can't relate to that mentality.

"I promise you that my husband will trouble you no further. And the threats of lawsuits and other things levied by your friends sealed Benedict's fate." She smiles with a touch of smugness. "He will be issuing a public apology in the House of Lords. The press will cover the event."

"Thank you, Annabelle," I say. "It means a lot that you came here to tell me in person."

"I am truly sorry for the trouble I've caused you. I'd hoped spending the night with you would make me feel better, especially since I'd heard about your…prowess from other women. But I felt horribly guilty afterward." She lowers her head, wringing her hands, but then meets my gaze again. "Telling Benedict about you was indefensible. I hoped he would realize he needs to try harder with me, but instead, he went after you. I don't expect or ask for your forgiveness."

"You don't need to ask. I forgive you, Annabelle."

She nods and gazes at me briefly, then walks away.

Avery shuts the door. "That was something."

"Yes."

"Why did you forgive her?"

"Because she's clearly suffered enough, just from living with the Duke."

Avery leans back against the door. "Do you think he'll really make things right?"

"Oh yes, I'm certain of that. Bullies are cowards at heart, and he won't want to risk losing his wife's fortune." I sling an arm around her waist to pull her into me. "But let's forget about the Duke and Duchess and go sightseeing with Derek. After all, he's going to be my brother-in-law. I should try to understand his bizarre American ways."

"What about work?"

"I texted Trudy while you were in the shower and informed her that we're taking the day off."

And we do exactly what I said. Avery, Derek, and I explore London and the countryside too, though we don't go all the way to Sommerleigh. Derek seems genuinely happy that Avery and I are engaged. He even suggests he might want to move to London to be closer to his sister and "soon-to-be, kind-of brother."

"There is a simple solution," I say. "You could follow Avery's lead. She's going to move her PR business to London. You could keep your company in New York but head up a new branch here."

Maybe Avery and I discussed her career plans in the shower this morning while we were shagging. But I know she meant what she said, especially since she jumped up and down and kissed every inch of my face when I called her plan a brilliant idea. Her business will no longer cater exclusively to the elites. She means to offer affordable alternatives for average people who want to avail themselves of her services, while still providing high-end options for her existing clientele.

"That's not a bad idea," Derek says. "Rich Brits probably need bodyguards even more than Americans do since you guys get into so much trouble."

"Naturally, wealthy Americans never get embroiled in scandals."

"Oh yeah, they do." Derek grins. "My business is going international. Might need advice from you and Avery about how to do that."

"Happy to help. We will be family soon."

In the afternoon, Evan MacTaggart rings to tell me the "business incubator" person wants to meet me at my office at nine tomorrow morning. I might've tossed and turned overnight, but I've earned the right to be anxious. The fate of Sommerleigh Sweets hangs in the balance.

At precisely nine o'clock, our visitor walks into the office.

I'm sitting behind the desk while Avery relaxes in one of the chairs opposite me.

Our guest shuts the door and marches over to my desk.

"Please come in," I say. Then I rise and offer my hand. "I'm Hugh Parrish, the Viscount Sommerleigh."

Our guest shakes my hand. "Diana Sangster. It's a pleasure to meet you, Lord Sommerleigh."

She's British, which surprises me because I'd sort of assumed my savior would be Scottish. A Scot did arrange this meeting. "Call me Hugh, please. And the lovely woman sitting over there is Avery Hahn, my fiancée and PR consultant."

Diana nods to Avery. "Evan MacTaggart told me about you, Ms. Hahn. I look forward to working with you."

"I understand you're a business incubator," I say, waving for her to take a seat while I do the same. "How does that work?"

"That's a hobby of mine." She crosses her legs and eyes me up and down. "But I don't want to shepherd your company or invest in it. I want to become your partner."

"What?"

"My capital, combined with my connections, can do more for Sommerleigh Sweets than merely provide distributors. I can turn this company into a powerhouse." She rests one hand on her knee and looks directly into my eyes. "Ask Evan if you don't believe me. References are always a good idea."

"Evan already gave you a glowing recommendation. But are you sure you want to become a partner in the company? After the blows we've suffered, it might take a long time to recover."

"Nonsense. Your business will be up and running again in no time."

"That sounds wonderful. We would love for you to join Sommerleigh Sweets." I want to interrogate Diana about her reasons for doing this, but I've suddenly remembered that thing about not looking a gift horse in the mouth. "I'll have the legal department draw up the paperwork."

"No need." She reaches into her attaché case and brings out a stapled set of papers, then she tosses it to me. The papers slide across the desktop toward me. "Have your solicitors look this over. But I assure you, my contracts are clear and concise and always fair."

My desk phone rings.

I pick it up. "Yes, Trudy?"

"Derek Hahn is here. I asked him to wait, but I thought you should know."

"Send him in. He should meet our guest."

Derek saunters into the room, halting near my desk. "What's up, boss?"

"Meet Diana Sangster. She is about to become our newest partner. Diana, this is Derek Hahn. We contract with him to provide security for Sommerleigh Sweets via his private firm. He's also Avery's brother."

Derek's gaze flicks to Diana, and his lips kink up at one corner. He shamelessly peruses her body until he at last meets her gaze. "Nice to meet you, Ms. Sangster."

"Call me Diana." She gives Derek the same perusal he had given her—and she smiles in the same way too. "I'm sure we will be seeing a great deal of each other."

"I'm at your service."

Why does it sound like he actually means "I'll fuck you anytime, anywhere"? She is a beautiful woman, so I can't blame him for trying it on. But in my office? During a meeting?

Diana swerves her attention to me. "I will require a bodyguard at all times. Might Mr. Hahn fulfill that role?"

"I'm sure Derek can assign one of his people—"

"No." She leans forward to stare at me with the sort of intensity I'd expect from ex-spy Logan MacTaggart, not from a business partner. "I want Mr. Hahn."

Avery seems puzzled, but her brother speaks up. "I'm happy to serve the lady."

Either I'm hallucinating or Derek meant "serve the lady" in a very unprofessional way.

Diana glides her tongue across her bottom lip while raking her gaze over Derek once more. "It's settled, then. I would like Mr. Hahn to accompany us on a tour of your headquarters as well as the factory."

"Of course," I tell her. "Are you available now, Derek?"

"Sure thing." He offers his arm to Diana. "Let me be your escort."

They walk out the door.

Avery and I lag a little behind the pair so we can talk without them hearing.

"Derek wants to shag her," I whisper. "Please tell me your brother has enough discretion not to ruin this entire deal."

"He's a professional bodyguard. Discretion is in his DNA." She gently elbows me in the side. "Unlike some people I know."

"Well, I can't argue that point. But I've changed."

"Yes, you have."

"After Diana leaves, we should visit a jeweler. Someone needs a ring."

My fiancée gives me a teasing look. "You want to call me?"

"No, I want to buy you a diamond ring."

"Just making sure. You Brits do say 'ring' when you mean 'call,' so I had reason to wonder."

I thread my fingers through hers. "You'll get used to the way we talk here. It's your home now."

She kisses my cheek. "Here with you is my forever home."

Want more of Derek and Diana? Experience their story in *One Hot Deal* (Hot Brits, Book Eight).

Love the

Hot Brits

series?

Visit
AnnaDurand.com

to subscribe to her newsletter
for updates on forthcoming books in this series
&
to receive free gifts for signing up!

*A*nna Durand is a bestselling, multi-award-winning author of contemporary and paranormal romance. Her books have earned bestseller status on every major retailer and wonderful reviews from readers around the world. But that's the boring spiel. Here are the really cool things you want to know about Anna!

Born on Lackland Air Force Base in Texas, Anna grew up moving here, there, and everywhere thanks to her dad's job as an instructor pilot. She's lived in Texas (twice), Mississippi, California (twice), Michigan (twice), and Alaska—and now Ohio.

As for her writing, Anna has always made up stories in her head, but she didn't write them down until her teen years. Those first awful books went into the trash can a few years later, though she learned a lot from those stories. Eventually, she would pen her first romance novel, the paranormal romance *Willpower*, and she's never looked back since.

Want even more details about Anna? Get access to her extended bio when you subscribe to her newsletter and download the free bonus ebook, *Hot Scots Confidential*. You'll also get hot deleted scenes, character interviews, fun facts, and more! Plus you'll receive the short story *Tempted by a Kiss* and mutliple bonus chapters in both ebook and audiobook formats.

Visit AnnaDurand.com to sign up.